PERORI

Paul McDermott

Published by Leaf by Leaf
an imprint of Cinnamon Press,
Office 49019, PO Box 15113, Birmingham, B2 2NJ
www.cinnamonpress.com

The right of Paul McDermott to be identified as author of this work has been asserted by him in accordance with the Copyright, Designs and Patent Act, 1988. © 2025, Paul McDermott.
Print Edition ISBN 978-1-78864-886-8

British Library Cataloguing in Publication Data. A CIP record for this book can be obtained from the British Library.

All rights reserved. No part of this publication may be reproduced, stored in a retrieval system, or in any form or by any means, electronic, mechanical, photocopying, recording or otherwise without the prior written permission of the publishers. This book may not be lent, hired out, resold or otherwise disposed of by way of trade in any form of binding or cover other than that in which it is published, without the prior consent of the publishers.

Designed and typeset in Adobe Caslon pro and Herculanum by Cinnamon Press. Celtic knot designs (c) Yulia Buchatskaya/iStock. Cover design by Adam Craig © Adam Craig.
Cinnamon Press is represented by Inpress.

ABOUT THE AUTHOR

By the time Paul McDermott got his first Adult library card (aged 11) he'd decided that he could do better than any of the authors available on the shelves of the Junior section, but as a callow youth with a fistful of A-levels he listened to his Head Teacher and went into teaching.

Twenty years of schools and five countries later, when he stopped 'chalking' he had an impressive mountain of notebooks filled with ideas, plot outlines, and the beginnings of several stories percolating, hinting at the untold gallons of coffee he'd consume while he turned them into finished books.

Paul describes himself as a 'moody writer' who will have several yarns in progress and work on the one he's in the mood for. It's a protection against writer's block, which might (or not) be as true as any of the fiction he writes. And some of his stories are closer to the Truth than others...

PERORI

CHAPTER ONE

Perori.

His meagre cloak was no defence against torrential rain, plastered so tightly to his body it could have been an extra skin. Even that would have been welcome had it also provided extra weatherproofing. Leaning heavily on his staff, the traveller paused and tried once more to peer further than a stone's cast in any direction.

Below his feet the ground dropped, crumbling and spooling treacherously under the relentless pressure of rain before decanting into the rising dark waters of the river forming the northern boundary of Mercia. On a day with better visibility he could have made out the opposite riverbank, less than a mile away even here at the widest point of the estuary. There was a vague suggestion of a defined shape at the corner of his vision—possibly the shelter he sought, sanctuary from the storm. Screwing his eyes tighter against the hissing stair rods of rain, he staggered a few yards further. There was only one logical place to build a warning tower. It had to be close to the western point of the promontory, guiding shipping looking for anchorage in the Pool. The monastery—and the monks who provided the ferry crossing must therefore be close.

He found the track by the simple method of stepping from a tussock and sinking to his knees in liquid mud.

Two parallel ruts stretched left and right. Turning left, keeping the roar of the swollen river on his right, he slopped slightly uphill to the barely perceived shadow he trusted to resolve into a building.

It could have been his imagination, but he sensed a slight lessening of power as the driving wind and rain swept before it. The darkness at the limit of his vision grew and solidified into a regular artefact. By degrees it became a middle-distance object before revealing itself in close-up. He could identify it as a solid, rough-built wall of dressed stone. He leant against it thankfully; the near absence of the howling gale was a relief as he stood in its lea.

"Now all you have to do," he adjured himself, "is find a gate, and hope there may be an ostiary alert enough to hear you, and sober enough to let you in."

Laying aside his staff, he wrung one-handed what excess water he could from his hair and beard. He replaced his largely ineffective head covering and felt his way along the blank wall to the nearest corner. Despite the difficulty of drying himself one-handed, he was unwilling or unable to use both hands for the purpose. His left hand and arm were immobile, at an odd angle, but from the curious way he held the cloak a chance observer would have been unable to decide if this was due to an injury or a burden.

"*Advenio… advenio!*"

The entrance gate faced east, protected from the worst ravages of the gale making its first landfall after thousands of miles across a cruel, frozen sea. Despite his brief respite, the supplicant barely had strength to remain upright as he pounded with his staff. A light snick and the briefest glance through the eye space was followed by bolts being released and the gate opened.

"*Deo gratias!*" was all he could manage as he stumbled, almost swooned, across the threshold and leaned heavily, unashamedly, on the doorward of the evening. His benefactor guided him in silence to a stool. A second monk, who had materialised just as silently, turned to one side and returned with warm, dry towels. As he rubbed a semblance of life back into his limbs, the supplicant wondered if he had chanced to beg succour from an order of Trappists, or perhaps others who had embraced a vow of silence; neither of those who had received him showed curiosity or inclination to initiate conversation.

An older, tonsured figure appeared silently. Neither monk could have seen him approaching from where they stood, but somehow sensed his advent and moved simultaneously to opposite sides of the entry nave to stand in semi-shadow.

"Thank you, Brother Gwyn, Brother Hywel. You may both retire: I will take responsibility for the remainder of the night watch."

Both the attentive statues inclined their heads briefly and moved off side by side, automatically matching step, still without a word. Their leather sandals flapped briefly; after a few seconds the quiet snick of a door latch was sensed rather than heard. When he stopped towelling his frozen ears, the only sound appeared to be his own breathing, preternaturally loud from the vigour and energy of his recent rough ministrations.

"My thanks, Father," he began to stutter through still-frozen lips.

With a light smile and a gentle shake of his head, the

cleric silenced him. "Do not overexert yourself: I can see you have endured bitter exposure in this late autumn storm! Time for civilities once you are somewhat restored, with dry clothing and what simple food we can provide at this hour. My name is Prior Asaph. Brother Gwyn, the ostiary, and Brother Hywel are young novices from Wales; they have recently joined the monastery. Their command of both Latin and English is still somewhat uncertain. I imagine that this is why they have opted to remain silent in your presence, rather than any monastic rule—or lack of courtesy on their part!"

With a simple hand gesture, Prior Asaph indicated that the unexpected guest should precede him out of the room, along the same passage Gwyn and Hywel had used. Unseen hands opened a door as they reached the end of the corridor and entered a kitchen which to his still-chilled body felt as warm as one of the lesser punishment cells of Hell. A selection of clean, dry clothing in varied sizes was laid for him. Warm bread, cheese, and a pitcher containing what proved to be a sweet, mulled wine were on a table to one side of the bright hearth fire.

An acolyte—presumably the one who had opened the door on his approach—came to assist with the removal of sodden outdoor clothing. As the cloak was taken from his shoulders he instinctively tensed, wrapping his left arm more securely around what he had been carrying, protecting it as well as he could from the worst effects of the foul weather he had stoically endured.

The burden was cocooned in layer on layer of expensive, rare leathers: a musical instrument of exceptional quality. This much was obvious without close inspection, and it was as certain that—in the right hands—this instrument would have a beauty and clarity to make legends of the lute and whoever was privileged to play it. Prior Asaph's ancient eyes missed nothing. He nodded, almost as if to himself.

"I can see your tale is not short. Clearly it must wait until you are rested and restored, so you may do it justice." He paused, an implied challenge in his tone, "I assume you are both willing and able to tell the tale, my son?"

The response was a grateful, exhausted nod. "I am already indebted for your charity this night, Prior Asaph. It would indeed be a churlish slur on the name Easten I am proud to bear were I to refuse. I thank you for your indulgence, as I have travelled far these last days, and will gladly repay your hospitality with an account of the history of the lute Perori, her powers, and the reason for my journey…"

CHAPTER TWO

Though it was pale, the late autumn sun rising above the line of the sill was enough to rouse Easten from his seemingly dreamless sleep—only a degree away from catalepsy. More than once, Prior Asaph had paused during his night rounds and checked carefully before being certain Easten was still breathing unaided.

He yawned and stretched, the oft-washed, softened fabric of the homespun habit he had been loaned comfortable against his skin. Opening his eyes, his first thought was for the lute he had persevered to protect through the previous night's downpour. It stood where he had left it, in the ingle to the left of the hearth, wrapped in the protective layers in which it was sealed for the journey. He relaxed, casting about the room. The storm had broken, and the day appeared as fair as any early summer morn—yet from the position of the sun, he sensed he had slept much later than was either wise or practical for most of the time he had been travelling. This, he felt, was a rare opportunity to relax, recoup both physically and spiritually before embarking on the next stage of his quest, which was likely to be the most dangerous.

A discreet knock, and the door of the room opened. A tonsured figure, little more than a boy of eleven or twelve, pushed it open with his hip and entered bearing a pile of towels almost as big as himself. Depositing these on a small table close to the hearth he returned to the passageway outside the door and carried in a large copper basin of steaming hot water, plus oils and cleansing materials. A silent bow and he was gone, closing the door softly behind.

During his ablutions, Easten sorted through a variety of scenarios. All had some significance for the next stage of his journey, some more positive or attractive than others. The major drawback that currently applied to each step without exception came back to one fact every time. Detail—or the lack thereof—concerning his current position as… honoured guest? minor irritation? or (God forbid!) a most unwelcome stranger who could expect a minimum of courtesy and no assistance whatsoever? Yet from what little he had seen and experienced of his hosts, he somehow doubted this would be the case.

As he towelled the last moisture from his neck, feeling the glow of improved circulation coursing under his skin, an errant draught made him spin round. His right hand dropped to where his skeán normally sat on his belt, before he relaxed and smiled apologetically at the monk whose habitually silent entrance had caused the draught from the door.

"*Mea culpa!*" he breathed, sincerely, and knew from the monk's stance he had made a sensible decision by addressing his visitor in Latin, the only lingua franca of the West.

This was not the young acolyte who had brought him towels and hot water, nor was it the senior Prior Asaph with whom he had spoken briefly when he claimed sanctuary from the storm. Young, certainly, but with something 'of the world' about him. Possibly late twenties, Easten thought, waiting for the newcomer to take the initiative.

The monk's young/old eyes missed nothing, and had noted Easten's instinctive reaction to being disturbed unexpectedly.

"You have been travelling alone for some time." A statement, not a question.

Easten nodded.

"Habits—good and bad—die hard, Father."

"You do me too much honour. My title is Brother: Brother Fergal. I have a number of years' study ahead before I can claim the title you so freely bestow."

Yet there was no hint of reprimand, and Easten sensed that he was in fact welcome, though unexpected, in this outpost of the realm. Straightening to his full height, he inclined his head and mustered as much dignity as possible for a half-clad man. "My name is Easten: what title I have must also serve as job description, for I am first and foremost Bard to… a certain lord, and charged with the deliverance of vital information to his cousin. That is my errand in these parts. I must find passage to Erin to complete my task."

"Bard, you say?" murmured Brother Fergal. For a moment Easten was unsure if he should respond, hearing the questioning lilt. Seeming oblivious of the hiatus, Fergal continued: "So can I better understand why you are so scrupulously careful of your burden: it is your preferred instrument, is it not? A… zither? lute? I confess I am not a musician and cannot identify one string instrument over another… but I can understand why a trained musician and one claiming the honoured title of Bard would be reluctant to leave behind an instrument of quality if he knew he would be absent for some considerable time."

Pulling on a jerkin, Easten realised he had instinctively positioned between his instrument and the… intruder? Surely some less negative description had been earned? Irrespective of his feelings that this was a secure place, in which he was safe from unexpected attack, Easten had lived on his wits for weeks and was still not prepared to trust others however friendly they might appear.

The significance of this dance had not escaped Brother Fergal, who now smiled again in a worldly-wise fashion. "Believe me, Bard Easten, there are none here would wish you ill: and many—myself first and foremost—who would be honoured if you would consent to…" he paused, seemingly embarrassed.

"…to provide some entertainment for you, perhaps?" Easten suggested, noting the self-conscious tinge in Fergal's visage as he dumbly nodded.

"That would be a small price for sanctuary and hospitality, Brother!" Easten added, "and when I have asked for the advice and assistance I shall need for the next stage of my quest, you will no doubt agree I will be in your debt for considerably more than the modest value of a few ballads!"

Apparently relieved that the negotiations had gone as well as he could have hoped for, Fergal made to withdraw.

"Prior Asaph enjoins you to break your fast with him in the Refectory after Matins. There is still time for you to join us, if you wish, for the service itself…" Easten sensed it would make a far better impression if he agreed to partake in the early service. He considered himself a Christian anyway, and opportunities to attend any services over the last few weeks had been few. Inclining his head, he followed Fergal from the chamber and along well-lit aisles to the chapel.

"*Ite, missa est!*"

"*Deo Gratias!*"

The soaring tones of the final benediction and response rang in Easten's ears and memory as he walked between Brother Fergal and Prior Asaph from the chapel to the refectory. The melody made the simple text a thing of beauty, a musical statement of belief. For a moment he wondered if he might possibly adapt it for a melody that had been lurking on the fringes of his imagination for days. He shuddered. The thought was uncomfortably close to blasphemy.

"Are you cold, my lord?"

Easten blinked, and returned to everyday practicalities. "Nay, Brother: I do but daydream: perhaps I might discuss private things with a confessor later this day?"

Brother Fergal averred that this might be easily arranged and led onwards to the first meal of the day. This transpired to be home-baked flatbread and a soupstew based on fresh-caught mussels.

"...and so, my Lord Prior, I was told in Deva that I might inquire about passage to my lord's kith in Erin from this Priory: and further, I would not be refused room and lodging should I need it. My thanks once more for the sanctuary you extended to me in last night's storm!"

"Yet you skate lightly over the nature of your—quest—and the urgency which has driven you far and fast through countryside that must have been unfamiliar to you... ah, rest easy, guest!"

Easten had become visibly agitated at the nuances in

the Prior's soft comments.

"…the nature of your movements, and your liege lord's intent in sending you are of no possible consequence to me or my brethren in this Priory! Politics and intrigue are terms we unfortunately must acknowledge as descriptions of human failings, but they have no significance for us simple men of God in this quiet backwater of the realm. Since the Romans retreated as their Empire crumbled almost eight hundred years ago, we have been allowed to…. arrange our own affairs, while acknowledging the authority of the Kings as they held sway in the land…"

Neither by tone nor inflection did Prior Asaph give any indication of approval or approbation of the concept of a secular monarch. Easten, however, sensed he was dealing with a proud and independent spirit. He nodded. "My liege has adjured me to speak as little as may be prudent regarding my journey, at least until I have managed to reach Erin and am close enough to his kinsman to call upon his assistance, should it be necessary. The matter is…" he hesitated.

"Delicate?" suggested Prior Asaph.

Somewhat surprised Easten shook his head. His next sentence caught Prior Asaph unprepared. "Prior Asaph, I said to Brother Fergal this morning I wished to speak to a confessor. Will you do me the honour, please? There is an aspect of my—quest, as you called it—which troubles me and I would be shriven before chancing my soul to the weather, and the seas I must now cross."

For answer Prior Asaph took a stole from a concealed fold on his robe, kissed it and placed it around his neck. Making the Sign of the Cross, he sat closer to Easten and waited.

"I must ask for your guidance and—I hope!—your blessing on the venture I have promised to fulfil as best I may in the service of my liege lord, to whom my fealty has always been unquestioned. I converted to the Faith as an adult, at Michaelmas five years ago. I try to live my life according to the guidance I was given before being received into the Church. I am aware that there are many… supposed charms and forgeries, presented as holy relics by charlatans and others who would happily gull all who can be persuaded to offer coin for their purse. But, Prior Asaph, the true purpose of my journey to my lord's kin in Erin is inextricably entwined with the… properties… the word lightly stressed "…of an object I bear with me." He paused. "And before you question me further," he added, "I can only aver as a musician of some little skill I am unable to provide a natural explanation for some of the things I myself have witnessed."

Carefully, reverently, he slowly peeled the protective layers of skins wrapped around his instrument.

"There is a long and wondrous tale concerning the lute Perori," he began, as he carefully stripped the final layer of coverings. Even in the dim, subdued lighting of the candles, it had a lustrous life of its own. The wood, carefully oiled and polished by countless pairs of caring bardic hands glowed with an antiquity and quality that could not be counterfeited. Even a non-musician such as Prior Asaph would sense without doubt that this was an instrument which, in the right hands, would sing true and with great power as well as unique beauty.

"Father, I…"

"Prior, my son. The title you honour me with is unearned."

"Prior Asaph. Forgive me, as a recent convert I think of all clerics as being the same! Still, I ask you hear me in the spirit of hearing a sinner making his confession. The history I tell includes much the Church may regard as heretical, even blasphemous, and I would be shriven of such faults before trusting myself and soul to the dangers of the sea voyage I must make to complete the task my lord has charged me. The lute Perori weaves a strange tale, part history, part legend. It is still, to my best knowledge, exclusively an oral tradition, for few amongst even the best educated lords in Gwynedd, Dyfed or other parts have learned their letters as yet: and until they do, we poor impoverished bards wait our turn also." Easten's wry smile robbed his words of any possible bitterness.

Easten continued, "Herein lies—at least in part—my reason for feeling a need to confess before I depart these shores on the most dangerous leg of my journey. Perori is credited with powers of an unnatural, even supernatural or magical nature. Things I myself have witnessed I cannot explain in any other way, and I am sorely troubled by what the Church may regard as either… miraculous… or blasphemy."

Prior Asaph nodded. "Your caution and your conscience speak well of you, as a bard and as a person who would know the truth in the events that unfold around each of us in our daily lives," he said, calmly. "Also: there are many things we cannot explain in the richness and diversity of life, but must perforce accept—often with a blind faith in the wisdom of One who is greater than us all. Does that make these things which we are unable to explain or understand, magical? Miraculous? Supernatural? Even… blasphemous?"

"I may not be that many years older than yourself, Easten, but I have heard countless confessions of faults—real and imagined!—from boys, men and women, too, over the years since I first took my vows. I too have both heard and seen things I cannot explain without terms such as you suggest, but that does not mean all these things are by their nature evil or have some 'wrongness' about them. It simply means we mere mortals do not yet have sufficient understanding to explain God's ways. Tell me as much of your story as you can," he paused, "or may… for I can appreciate your liege lord has charged you with a certain amount of secrecy he deems necessary for the success of your mission. I have no wish to place you in a cleft stick between explaining yourself to me and going against your master's wishes!"

Relieved, Easten nodded his sincere thanks. "Perori has passed from senior Bard to senior Bard for generations; almost a badge of office, for without the best instrument to play, what musician could claim to be more than a barely sufficient journeyman? For as you must surely know, Prior—since your neighbours to the south are the clans of Gwynedd—the title of Bard is more than a mere courtesy: it is an honour to be earned, and earned on merit alone!"

He stroked the instrument, with reverence. It was an automatic gesture, and Easten was evidently unaware of the movement. "Every guardian of this lute—and yes, I include myself—has borne witness to one occasion, sometimes several, when… Prior Asaph, this sounds ridiculous, I know: is it possible for such an object of beauty to be… an instrument of Peace?"

Whatever Prior Asaph might have expected, it was not

this. His mind raced, and he felt his heart briefly skip a single stroke as he tried to assess the implications the tale his guest appeared to be telling might reveal.

"If indeed the lute Perori has been a… positive influence of such a nature, bard Easten, then surely it can only be on 'the side of the angels'. And you can have no fears of any sin involved in your giving me a full and truthful account of your personal experiences, or any other occurrences you feel are well documented and will stand the ultimate test of Truth."

Easten nodded his acceptance of this guarded but open encouragement, and continued: "Prior, I have led a somewhat sheltered existence thus far in the service of my Lord Caradoc. This journey I make on his behalf is the first time in my thirty years I travelled more than a day's journey from the town in which I was born, Caerleon."

"Isca Silura," murmured the Prior, automatically, then smiled at the blank expression on his guest's face.

"That was the name which the invading Romans gave the settlement, and the one still given in the few written histories we have: for they are all in the Roman tongue, the lingua franca of scribes, priests and historians. The fortress town close by that you must have passed on your journey still uses its Roman name, Deva. Pray, continue."

"I received the badge of my calling when I sang my way to favour at the Eisteddfod and was thus chosen by Lord Caradoc to be his bard. The post had been vacant some time following the death of the previous bard, and the lute had perforce remained sealed and protected, but unused."

"The first thing I noticed when I peeled back the coverings was how light and resilient it was. But at the same time…" he leaned forward for emphasis, and all but breathed: "...at the same time, it remained in perfect true pitch!"

He sat back, awaiting Prior Asaph's reaction. After a few seconds, a puzzled frown crossed his face, rapidly followed by a look of chagrin. "My apologies, Prior, why indeed should you know? You have already told me you are not a musician! Well, then, any stringed instrument needs constant attention and tuning—especially when laid aside for any length of time without being played regularly. It should not be possible to lay aside a lute, or any other instrument of this nature, and expect it to remain in tune and playable after almost two years."

"A minor miracle indeed, on the face of it," agreed Prior Asaph, "but I assume there is more to tell?"

Easten nodded. "Indeed there is, Fa... Prior," he amended himself swiftly, with a self-conscious grin. "From the first, it was as though it moulded itself to me like a boot or other pieces of attire specially tailored to me, and me alone.

"I come from a modest background. My family is not wealthy. Neither I nor my father could have afforded to purchase such an instrument, though it was evident as a young boy I had talent for music. I had instruction in the techniques of play for the lute and other common instruments in the years I could study, though even those lessons I fear cost my father more than he could easily afford: but at least he saw me win the Eisteddfod and my placement at court before he died.

"I began to feel almost as if Perori was playing me, rather than I her. My fingers seemed to find the right stops, or the most pleasant sweeps and strums without me having to think about it: me, who had never been able to afford more than a few cheap, quickly-made (and just as quickly broken!) reeds and pipes, barely more than toys that might amuse children a day or two at most!

"Soon I found if I sat and played, music would often come unbidden to my fingers, original melodies I knew I had never heard: and as I played—or was played—more often lyrics to fit the melody would fill my head, and I simply had to utter them or burst. To me, this was as much a miracle as the previous experience, as up to then I would always struggle with original words to a melody."

He stirred. "Prior Asaph, to you these things will sound perhaps coincidence, pleasing in themselves but not more than the natural development of a musician's art. But there were events on my journey, too many to recall in detail for they occurred almost every single day. They cannot be explained away as coincidence and good fortune, they are far too numerous for that!

"On my very first day, at the first village I came to, a large and mean-looking wolflike dog rocketed past me chasing a mangy, flea-bitten cat. When silence fell, I glanced back—to see the pair lying side by side, licking and grooming each other as if this were the only existence either of them had ever known.

"That evening, I walked into a hostel to ask about a bed for the night. Two large, muscled types faced each other in a cleared space inside the door, each with a knife in his hand and murder in his mind.

"As I pushed at the door Perori must have nudged the doorjamb gently, for I felt (rather than heard) the faintest of chimes from her strings. It was as if the sworn enemies of the moment also heard something, for they both shook their heads as one does to shoo an annoying fly, then sheathed their knives, offered each other the most sincere apologies, and sat to drink together.

"These things may seem small and unimportant individually, Prior: but they have been constantly with me throughout my northward journey, part of the warp and weft of my day. I can no longer ignore them as chance events."

"Nor can you credit the possibility of Divine Intervention in such small matters," Prior Asaph remarked, calmly and without seeming to pass judgement, "but what of the alternative possibility of some darker, older, pagan superstition, perhaps involving a form of magic? Have you considered that?"

The Prior's words hung in the air, almost but not quite visible between them. Not trusting himself to speak, Easten nodded confirmation.

"Which, I take it, you think would not be well received by a… a man of the cloth such as myself." There was no hint of a question in Prior Asaph's voice, rather a calm statement of fact. "My son, there is no guilt in you thinking as you do, especially on a long and lonely journey with no travelling companion to confide in—or to confirm that what you believe you have seen has not been illusion, either in part or in its entirety. No, I do not disbelieve what you have told me, far from it! I am simply pointing out that if you had someone to discuss these things with, you might be in an easier state of mind at the moment!"

"You do believe me, then?" Easten exclaimed, relief evident in his voice.

"Young man, I do not believe you are capable of dissembling, even if you wished to do so! Your honesty is clear in all that you have told me—and, more important, in the way you tell your tale! You have truly chosen the right profession, Bard! If your singing voice matches your taletelling skills, I believe you could charm the birds out of the treetops if you so choose!"

"I told you before that if this marvellous instrument has shown signs of mediating peace in an uncertain world, it can only be counted as a boon, a blessing, something we may not as yet understand but must consider a sign of sorts—and most certainly something we may have sore need of, in the present troubled times.

"You gave the instrument a name, as if it were a living entity: Perori?"

"Yes, Prior. This is not, I hope, something which offends the Church: but truly great instruments—and as a musician, I can assure you that this lute deserves the description!—have traditionally always been given names by musicians honoured to possess them for a brief lifetime of playing before they are given further to another player. I am the tenth documented holder of the privilege of playing Perori: it is at very least a century since she was created... Your pardon, Prior! I did not mean to sound..."

Prior Asaph smiled. "An object of true beauty can indeed appear to possess individuality: it can even appear to have a vibrant independent life. It is no sin to think in such terms, my son. Someone in such an honourable profession as you have chosen would be less than human if he did not think of such a fine instrument as having lifelike qualities."

Easten's respect for this astute man of the cloth deepened. He was not, Easten realised, an isolated, dreamy person who had opted to ignore the world for the life of the cloisters. How, he wondered, could he appear so worldly-wise?

As if following Easten's thoughts, Prior Asaph smiled. "I travelled and saw a great many things of the world before I felt the call of the Church. I believe I can understand how a sensitive and accomplished musician such as yourself would react to an exquisite, finely made instrument. There can be no shame or sin in admiring beauty: it is merely recognition of the skill of the craftsman, who in turn has received his skills from the Creator of us all. Do you have aught else on your conscience?"

Startled by the question, Easten gathered his wits and accounted for himself, listing minor peccadilloes of hastiness and anger he felt he had been guilty of on his journey thus far. As the Prior murmured the familiar words of the *Te Absolvo*, Easten planned the way he would broach the assistance he hoped to obtain.

"Would you consent to demonstrate your skills on this wondrous instrument, after our midday repast?"

Swiftly coming to the conclusion of his final Ave Maria, Easten nodded gladly. This was perhaps the opening he sought, an opportunity to barter his skills for the favour.

"If my skills, such as they are, may please your community I will be glad to perform something suitable. I am already indebted to you for sanctuary from the elements. I have a further boon to ask in the form of advice, so the fee you ask of me in return is little enough! It would be an honour to repay your hospitality in this way!"

Prior Asaph raised his eyebrows at Easten's mention of

another favour. He made no comment, but nodded gravely. "Let the day bring forth what it will," he proclaimed, rising to indicate that the confession and interview had reached its conclusion. "I must be about my daily office, and you may if you wish avail yourself of our small library, or utilise the time until the noon-bell rings for private reflection in your…" he paused briefly before concluding: "…a visiting religious would not take the term 'your cell' amiss, but I would be sure that the term does not have another less pleasant association for a secular guest?"

Easten smiled. "I too have some experience with other walks of life, Prior, and am too grateful for your hospitality thus far to take umbrage at any term you care to use for the shelter you have already provided! If it would not offend or inconvenience anyone, I would like your permission to rehearse some pieces in the room, if it will not disturb anyone at prayer?"

Prior Asaph assured Easten this would be perfectly acceptable, and escorted his guest back to his temporary lodging, then departed to resume his daily routines.

CHAPTER THREE

Glancing out of the window, Easten gave himself an hour before the noon-bell was due to be rung. Carefully stripping the layers of protective valise from Perori, he sat and gave himself to a careful scrutiny of the instrument, an examination that was also an opportunity to polish it, and assure himself it had taken no harm on the journey.

The smooth, repetitive actions of cleaning and polishing calmed him; before long this became automatic while his mind raced with other considerations. Rapt, he barely noticed when his hands ceased to polish and caress the smooth maple and elegant rosewood inlays of his beloved Perori. Half dreaming, he played short riffs and phrases of melody that grew ever more complex, and built into a more formal melodic line. As he became aware of this, Easten concentrated on altering and refining the shape of the melody, recognising it was inspired by the Ave Maria he had heard in the chapel earlier that day.

As he intoned the final line "…*nunc et in hora mortis…*" he surfaced to the world once more and discovered he had acquired an audience. An (as yet untonsured) novice, probably younger than Easten, stood open-mouthed at the door, which he now noticed must have been ajar since Prior Asaph's departure. Bringing his composition to a graceful conclusion with a satisfying, embellished plagal cadence to mark the final "Amen", Easten laid the instrument carefully on one side and smiled an encouraging greeting to reassure his visitor. The young man appeared nervous and overawed by the Priory's unexpected guest, or by the intricacies of the music.

"Enter, and welcome!" He repeated his greeting in Latin to avoid misunderstanding.

"My grateful thanks, sire: it is long since I last heard such beautiful music." The lilt in this man's voice was pleasant, but not one Easten could identify.

"I am named Brion, my lord, and am but newly arrived from my master Cormac's halls in Teamhair."

At once, Easten placed the accent. "Teamhair: is that not also called Tara, across the sea to the west?"

"It is, my lord."

"Please! I am neither Lord nor Sire, but a traveller on my master's bidding! Yet it is strange we should meet here…"

"Your playing is that of a true master, and your lute of surpassing quality."

"I am blessed with a patron generous in the support he has given my modest talent: the instrument he provided me as part of my hire. But to meet one who hails from Teamhair, or Tara, is a happy matter. It would fit well with my purpose if I might persuade you to travel with me, as I may have sore need of one who can assist with language from time to time. My knowledge of the Gael is limited to what I have heard travelling through Cymru—and I am told the two languages, while similar, are not interchangeable. My name is Easten, and if I might have your hand on it I would ask Prior Asaph for your companionship when I continue my journey?"

A curious expression crossed Brion's face before he

replied, gravely: "Indeed, I would be honoured to be of service to you, when you journey onwards! If my knowledge of Tara and what language skills I possess can be of some use, Prior Asaph may be swayed to agree to your request." He paused. "It would not… displease me… to visit my home and my family." Again, there was a flicker of conflict in his eyes.

Easten was astute enough to recognise it, and politic enough not to refer to it. "I understand: your duty, as a religious man, must foremost be to your order and your… Brother Superior? Is that the correct title?"

Brion smiled. "Prior Asaph is not one to insist on a title! In this house we do not stand on ceremony, or follow a rigid Rule! Prior Asaph may be obliged to decide on the best of a number of possibilities, but many things are decided by consent, and after a suitable period of prayer and reflection. But I was sent to speak to you on another matter; the weather is much improved, and if you wish to lay aside your lute a short while, I would show you the grounds of our Priory."

Easten nodded. Returning the lute to its silken cocoon—mercifully spared the ravages of the foul weather during the latter stages of his journey thanks to the sturdy weatherproofing of the outer layers—he laid it carefully on his cot and followed Brion along two short corridors and one longer passage to a sturdy door in what he assumed to be the outer wall of the main building.

The door nestled on the jamb, and there was not the slightest chink or space for a draught . As Brion opened the door, bright sunlight flooded the space and Easten discovered how accustomed his eyes had become to the subdued lighting of the candles in his room and in the priory passages. Mid-morning sunlight dazzled him, and he had to squint until his eyes adjusted to natural light levels.

They were in a walled cloister, square and of goodly proportions. Narrow paths ran the perimeter and it was bisected by two diagonal walks. Each of the triangular beds thus formed was filled with green plant life, and Easten recognised this was an important part of the priory's provisions store, herb garden and apothecary all in one carefully tended plot. Herbs, spices and medicinal plants abounded, and the mingling scents were almost overpowering in the still conditions the surrounding walls created. The walls, he noted, were utilised to provide growing frames for plants that could be adapted to climb rather than spread: he recognised rose hips, and varieties of nut bush.

"Such a rich harvest!" he breathed, savouring the blend of aromas.

"You are well provided, both in medical herbs and for savoury dishes through the lean winter months!"

"Indeed we are—yet there are travellers who might not recognise what they see here, thinking it an extravagance of poorly controlled weeds."

"I see here many plants I have come to learn may have several uses, according to how they are prepared," replied Easten. "Take this mint, which may be brewed as a tea, aiding digestion, or infused in spirit as a means of making the toughest mutton taste as good as young spring lamb!"

Brion smiled. "I see you have a depth of knowledge outside the remit of a journeyman musician! Come, let me show you more of our way of life…"

The tour of Birkhead Priory was brief enough, as the

priory was compact, practical in form rather than intended to impress. Well-nourished cattle and sheep dotted the lush fields surrounding the building, and beyond row on row of grain and pulse crops.

The priory also boasted an ingenious heating system, a legacy from Roman occupation tended and cared for continuously since the Empire's collapse. This meant a continuous supply of heated water for bathing. There was also a steam room: and surplus heat from the fires required to produce the hot water was carefully vented to ensure the herb and spice garden was never subject to sudden seed-killing winter frosts. Easten's attention was caught by a patch of unexpected colour at the edge of his vision. Shading his eyes, he gazed north, with the sun fast approaching its zenith. Brion followed the direction of his guest's interest.

"You have noticed our ferryman," he observed, waiting for Easten's response.

"Ferryman? I understand the term, but…"

"Living as we do, on the banks of a river that widens rapidly and disgorges into the sea, we must adapt to conditions as we find them. Much of the trading and barter we must perform for what we cannot produce ourselves is done with neighbours living on the northern shore. For the most part they have no Latin and only a vague grasp of the Gospels, but they are honest, dependable people and share our affinity for boating. Indeed, they are masters in boatbuilding, and often make longer voyages at sea, in craft bigger than any we could handle."

Easten saw a possible solution to the problem of the next stage of his quest, and the request he must soon make of Prior Asaph: but at that moment the chapel bell announced the midday service, and so he followed Brion's lead and returned to the main building, where he could postpone further deliberations on his personal requests until the Mass was over and they had eaten lunch.

Anticipating a musical interlude following the meal, Prior Asaph had indicated that the Mass should not be the full, formal sung Mass of the day but the shorter form, unaccompanied by song other than the minimal Plainchant used for the Consecration of the Host and the *Ite Missa Est* dismissal.

The meal was simple, but not frugal. Easten noted the quality of the fresh home-grown vegetables was superior to that in many of the hostelries and manor homes where he had sung for his supper on the earlier part of his journey. This was also the case with the cheeses and breads he assumed were produced within the priory walls.

Once the tables had been cleared and Thanksgiving sung, Easten's fingers itched to demonstrate his instrument's purity of tone. An atmosphere of calm serenity, spiced with anticipation, settled on the dining area as the monks composed—most sitting in a relaxed position, hands in laps—awaiting Easten's performance.

Easten sensed the occasion merited formal introduction.

"We of the Welsh marches are not given to... idolatry, or other pagan beliefs... but there is an ancient and honourable tradition amongst bards and musicians, dating many generations before the Word of the Saviour reached these shores. According to this tradition, a truly remarkable instrument in its sweetness and tone, especially in the hands of a competent performer, is regarded as more than… mere gut wound on wood, and honoured with a name to indicate we consider it worthy of respect, having independent quality about it which places it close to a living, breathing entity in its own right."

He paused, looking to see if he had unwittingly offended anyone. Heartened this appeared not to be the case, he continued:

"I have the honour to have such an instrument in my possession. It was built by a master craftsman three, possibly four generations since, and has been accorded the name Perori. In Welsh, the name means quite simply: Music."

He deemed it unnecessary, even inappropriate, to add more in explanation, and concentrated on coaxing the best out of his instrument. In seconds, he was absorbed. A troop of mounted knights could have charged through the refectory and he would have been unaware. He relaxed and let his fingers pick out the comfortable, well-known cadences of the standard chants and melodies common in services. He sensed the familiar melodies would establish a sympathetic bond with his audience, and from the reactions he saw limned in their faces was gratified. Tensing at the audacity of what he had planned next, he subtly altered the rhythm his fingers plucked: the melody of the Ave Maria he had been extemporising when Brion first visited his lodgings throbbed soulfully around the room. There was no pause from one melody to the next, and he saw from the faces of his audience they were aware of the changes as they followed, one after another.

He built variations on the theme, adding a counterpoint in the tenor register that was almost an independent melody. Varying expressions of wonder and amazement were to be seen without exception in every face: he buried himself again in his craft, concentrating on the chords and arpeggios his fingers constructed and set in place without conscious effort.

"*Ora pro nobis… nunc et in hora mortis…* Pray for us… now and at the hour of our death."

As he came to the last line of the prayer and modulated the Plagal Cadence that signified the end of prayer, Easten became aware of his surroundings.

The silence was absolute. Even the crackling of dry wood in the hearth seemed preternaturally loud. Not even a deeply-drawn breath could be heard. For a moment Easten wondered if he had erred on what this secluded order of monks might permit in the name of Art. Had he unwittingly strayed beyond some unwritten but clear line of demarcation between good taste and heretical secularity? Prior Asaph rose from his seat and bowed as if in prayer. When he straightened, to Easten's unutterable relief, he was smiling warmly.

"Exquisite, my son!" he murmured, and approached to place his hands on Easten's shoulders in benediction. Murmurs of appreciation and thanks arose from the assembled monks, though they remained seated in deference to Asaph's seniority.

"How long have you been practicing that Ave?" Prior Asaph inquired as he released Easten from his embrace.

"I heard it for the first time this morning."

Prior Asaph stared in open disbelief. "Surely you had heard it before?"

"On my soul, Prior Asaph: I would remember if I had, and have no cause to lie to you or anyone! 'Tis certain; this morning was the first I have heard that musical setting, though I know the text well enough!" This afterthought brought a smile to the lips of more than one monk, including Prior Asaph's: the most common penitence was the recital of a number of Paters and Aves, according to the seriousness (or otherwise) of the confessed transgressions.

"Well, young man, it is clear you have been gifted with a most precious Talent by the Maker of us all, and have used the Talent wisely, as blessed Matthew says we should! Come, we have much to talk about, and I hope you may be persuaded to play for us again before you feel obliged to continue your journey... I am correct in assuming your goal lies beyond our humble priory?"

"I am already indebted to you for sanctuary from last night's storm, Prior, but will gladly play as often as you wish before my duties oblige me towards my destination. Perhaps we might speak of that in private?" So far as he knew, there was no reason he might not speak openly of his quest before the brothers, but an instinct that had already helped him avoid difficult situations made Easten cautious about disclosing his master's business too openly.

A curious expression crossed the Prior's face, gone so swiftly Easten was uncertain he had imagined it or not. With a graceful gesture and the merest bow, Prior Asaph indicated Easten precede him out of the refectory. Once the door was closed behind them, the Prior led along short, well-lit passages to a heavy oaken door, hung on sturdy iron hinges. It appeared to lack any key or locking mechanism, but after they passed though the arch and closed it, Easten understood. Although it could be locked (and barred) from the inside, its construction possessed neither keyhole nor other inbuilt weakness to enable a determined assailant to gain entry. Prior Asaph followed Easten's glance.

"This priory was well planned, and generously endowed by a wealthy patron who, according to the records, thought to buy himself indulgences for… certain excesses earlier in life.

"When completed, he decided it was wisest, most politic, to take up residence within the Priory. It was, after all, the strongest building for miles, and he had annoyed many of his closest neighbours. In his final years, he took Holy Orders and lived the life of a hermit, rarely venturing out of this room and never beyond the inner courtyard of the kitchen gardens."

"Which is why this door can only be locked and unlocked from the inside!" concluded Easten, amused but also saddened at the thought that such a decision could be forced on somebody by the debauched manner he had chosen to live.

"Very observant, for one so young!" commented Prior Asaph. "Now tell me: what is it that concerns you so much you wish to speak of it in private? Is it a matter for a confessional?" he said, indicating a stole hanging next to a breviary on a side table.

"No, my conscience is clear enough—at least, as regards my liege lord's business!" replied Easten with a short laugh. He had decided he liked as well as respected Prior Asaph and could entrust him with the details of why he must travel onwards. "Prior Asaph, my master has enjoined me to make my way to his kith at an Teamhair, or Tara, in Ireland, and to do so swiftly but discreetly.

"There I am to beseech his cousin to raise and send as many men as he may spare against raiders. Wild |

Fensmen from both east and west of my lord's manor attack constantly. His estate straddles a disputed tract where both the English and the Welsh language hold equal sway, and allegiance to any king or prince who holds court in a distant part of the land is of lesser import than loyalty to one's own liege lord."

"And so here you are; in effect, asking me—a humble servant of the Prince of Peace—to assist you in preparing an act of war against your lord's enemies?"

Prior Asaph's unexpected counter-thrust unsettled Easten; he flashed an angry riposte. "Nay, good Prior, not an act of war! My lord feels his family and retainers under threat from marauders who have no claim on his estate: he feels he has a duty to protect blood relatives who ask for his succour, and those who work for him on the estate! But to do this effectively, he needs must ask other members of his family for a show of strength, an armed presence to persuade this rabble to slink back to their mudflats and desist!

"And at the same time," he continued, in a softer tone "Remember what I said earlier on about my feeling that Perori is in some way intended as an instrument of peace. I tried to explain to you about some curious incidents on our journey, and it is my hope I might learn more of her powers of persuasion on my travels, possibly even guidance from the family shaman at Tara…"

Prior Asaph's brows contracted on hearing this evidently unfamiliar term.

"Your pardon, Prior Asaph, if the term 'shaman' is not in common usage. Amongst the Celtic tribes in Wales and in Eire it is an honourable title given to a learned elder, often one skilled in healing and—sometimes—a certain modest skill in augury."

Prior Asaph nodded.

"While we who consider ourselves to be followers of the Path of the Redeemer do not place trust in auguries and foretellings, I have heard the term and understand the traditions of the Celt nation, perhaps better than you might believe! For while it is true only God can know for certain what may befall tomorrow, there are yet ways a wise man may try to judge what the next day may bring, and from that plan for the most likely sequence of events."

Easten stared, open-mouthed. Though the contact he had had with priests and clerics was limited, he had not expected even this guarded degree of acceptance from the Prior. In his experience, the young Christian faith in its struggle to establish itself was inclined to denounce every trace of earlier religions.

"My son, how great is the difference between your shaman and Isaiah or one of the other prophets? Society has always found a way of honouring older, wiser heads with a title!"

Easten relaxed yet again: now he felt he could open his heart to the Prior and receive a fair hearing. "Throughout my journey I have felt a growing affinity with Perori, and I am convinced this superb instrument can prove to be, literally, an 'instrument for peace'—but how is beyond my ability to guess.

"The shaman at Tara is reputed to have forgotten his actual age, but he is ancient of days and was in his youth also a renowned bard whose fame was legend throughout Eire's Seven Kingdoms. Once I have fulfilled the obligation my liege lord has laid on me, I hope to ask for guidance from the shaman before I return. If I can offer my lord the prospect of a lasting peace, I know he would prefer that to further fighting!"

"You said you had a boon or favour to ask: how, then, might I be able to help you with your goal of brokering a peaceful resolution of the… difficulties you left behind on the Welsh borders?"

"Brion—the brother who was my guide this morning—mentioned the special relationship you have with the ferryman, and the boatbuilders who live on the north bank of the river.

"He told me that they build vessels which can safely cross to Eire. Prior Asaph, if you could possibly ask them to grant passage there and back—preferably providing passage for the force of arms I am to try and raise—my lord is a fair man and promised he will not stint in rewarding any assistance he is offered!"

Prior Asaph appreciated the diplomacy. "You would use a hired army to teach your enemy peace?" He smiled, adding hastily, "In truth, that sounds like drastic measures! Yet, I understand your reasoning! I will introduce you to our ferryman. He can help explain your request to the leaders of their community; you can then explain for them the terms your master is prepared to offer."

"And at the same time, you are not actively encouraging any 'act of war' as you described it!" added Easten with a grin. "Prior Asaph, I thank you with all my heart: if your neighbours across the river are as helpful as you have been, the success of my mission to Eire seems more likely than I dared hope!"

*

The ferryman was presented to Easten that afternoon: a short, bearded man whose shoulder muscles were his most prominent feature: evidence of how he spent most of each day sculling back and forth on the river Maere's inconstant tides and currents. When he was introduced, Easten felt obliged to ask if "Roar" was a name, or a job title.

"It may serve for both!" replied Prior Asaph, with a smile: "…for amongst his folk it is common for an artisan to take the name of a trade or natural skill: personal names among those of Norse lineage are almost always reserved for leaders and chieftains!"

"Northmen? Are these, then, a colony of Viking raiders?" Easten asked, with an unease in his voice. He had heard tales of the *berserkergang* seaborne raiders from the North, and felt some reservations about entrusting his safety to them for a voyage across a short but temperamental sea.

Prior Asaph laughed. "These people I can vouch for myself. Whatever stories you may have heard tell about the wildness and cruelty of Viking marauders are probably embroidered to frighten young children, and no more than distant memories now.

"These folk settled on the north banks of the Maere generations ago and put down roots, laying out farms and smallholdings as well as shipyards. They enjoy sailing, and are skilled seafarers, but sail only as far as they needs must to catch fish or from time-to-time trade with their relatives and brethren in Eire, and some small islands to the west."

Asaph turned to Roar and spoke to him rapidly in a language Easten assumed to be Norse. He seemed amused by what he heard, as he roared with laughter at the end of the story and approached Easten, clasping his hands around Easten's elbows in an unmistakeable gesture of acceptance.

"Come! We sail! River is…" he looked at Prior Asaph, evidently uncertain of the exact word he needed.

"I think he means, the tide is right to make a crossing if you leave now: he can have you back again this evening, should you wish it, to eat and sleep here in the Priory, but you may choose to remain with his people for the night. Whatever you decide, you will be safe with them: they are good folk!"

"Yes! River—tide! We sail now!" Roar was clearly eager to leave as soon as possible to take advantage of the tide. Leaving the Priory, carrying Perori carefully swathed in oilskins again, and under the watchful eye of Prior Asaph, Easten followed Roar out of the Priory and down to the wooden platform on the riverbank that served as a ferry point.

"*Sæd … stille!*" Roar told Easten, who needed little imagination to translate this Nordic command and strove to do so in the (to his eyes) minute and flimsy coracle, evidently their river transport. Despite the discomfort and doubts about the vessel's seaworthiness, his craftsman's eye scanned and judged as he clung limpet-like to the thwart that appeared to stiffen the longer flanks of the egg-shaped vessel as well as providing a seat of sorts for a passenger. A light frame of wicker or willow, he noted, was lapped with long, even strips of some durable bark, caulked and made watertight with further layers of a hide or other animal skin. Even with the ballast of two adults, it drew little draught and was evidently intended to skip lightly over the surface of a pond or river: it was certainly not intended for the rough and tumble of the open sea.

"Water... push—*hjælp*" explained Roar, using his hands to indicate that the direction of the incoming tide would balance the river's westward flow, enabling them to cross to the opposite bank without being pushed off course by wayward currents. Privately, Easten thought this somewhat optimistic, but he had no alternative: if he wished to negotiate with the leaders of this tribe of boatsmen, he was obliged to entrust himself to the skills of this ferryman, whom he could barely understand.

Offering a silent prayer to his new-found God (mixed with a few exhortations to some of the major deities he had professed before turning to Christian teaching) he settled as best he could for the crossing. From his low vantage, scant inches above the tiny waves that made the vessel bob alarmingly, the northern bank of the river seemed impossibly far. The day was clear and bright, but as far as Easten could tell they made little headway. When he glanced back, however, he saw that the priory jetty and the shore on which it stood was quickly dropping further astern.

Roar's strongly formed shoulder muscles drove rhythmically at the paddle, and the coracle skimmed smoothly in the 'dead hole' caused by the confluence of the fresh river water meeting the salt of the rising tide. It occurred to Easten that, if the few words that had (with difficulty) been exchanged between himself and the ferryman were a guide, he might have problems communicating his needs to the chieftain of the people he was about to meet. As a bard, his education was better than most. He could make himself understood in several dialects and recognised languages, though Latin was still the preferred lingua franca for educated people throughout what remained of the Roman Empire's onetime sphere of influence.

An alteration in the vessel's motion brought him back to full awareness of his surroundings. A bend upstream from their position meant they had reached a still, almost pond-like stretch of water and Roar could relax, easing his shoulder muscles but not showing obvious signs of undue exertion. Easten wondered if he could ever hope to be just as fresh after sculling a vessel and passenger cross-current for a distance of… how far was it, he wondered. Squinting into the haze, he estimated it to be at least mille passus in the Roman measurement—a term transmogrified to 'mile' by the English tongue. Roar tucked his oar under one arm and continued to sweep easily and rhythmically, but with less effort now they were out of the main current. Standing at his ease with one foot raised to perch on the boat's rim, he caught Easten's attention.

A certain amount of sign language gave Easten clues to what Roar was trying to get across.

"*Du… praata… Errrikk?*"

The first word (accompanied by a pointed finger) was not too far removed from Latin: Easten was in no doubt, therefore, he was being addressed. The second word was accompanied by Roar's hand next to his mouth, opening and closing rapidly, like a duck: Easten realised it must have something to do with "speaking" or "talking".

With the third word, Roar pointed towards the bank that by now was not far. Guessing that this was probably someone's name, Easten nodded and smiled, hoping the ferryman would recognise these basic gestures that seemed to have the same or similar meanings in every society. Minimal contact had been made; this seemed to satisfy Roar, who gave his attention to safely beaching the vessel.

Easten peered over the side. There was little to see: the vegetation beneath the surface, and even the water, were somehow darker here than on the southern riverbank. The vessel grounded in the final few inches depth of water, and Easten helped Roar carry the coracle safely above the line of seaweed that indicated a high-water mark, depositing it keel upward among sturdy bushes.

Roar looked back across the river, then indicated the direction they must walk. Easten understood "vi…" as meaning "we", and the "*gaar…* " (accompanied by fingers making a 'walking' movement) to indicate how they would continue their journey. He had the impression (but not the certainty) that Roar estimated the distance was about the same as they had travelled by boat.

"*Errik prata…*" (the 'duck' sign, next to the mouth again) "…gut." Now Easten was getting a 'feel' for this: 'gut' was so close to 'good' he recognised from several Saxon dialects he was certain he was understanding more with each attempt.

"Erik… speaks?… *praata*?… good? languages?"

Was he making himself understood, he wondered, introducing the concept of "more than one language" at this early stage. But it was important. He had little time for communication difficulties.

"La… lan…" Roar was obviously struggling.

Inspired, Easten grasped his own tongue between two fingers and began a pantomime of someone having difficulty with this body part. Roar nodded, holding his own tongue and dancing round laughing. Easten did the same for a few moments; then both stopped and looked at each other with more understanding. Closing his eyes, Roar mimicked a monk walking and singing.

"Erik *praata*," he said, nodding. Easten took this to mean that Erik—the clan leader, presumably—spoke some Latin. Relief flooded him.

"*Vi gaar.*" This was no longer a request; it had more urgency.

Easten looked up. The afternoon was advanced, and although the weather was set fair; it was as well not to chance travelling into the late evening and risk missing the path. "*Vi gaar*," he agreed, and they continued their journey.

Easten soon realised his concerns about missing the path were groundless. Through sandy hillocks held with tough speargrass, the track from the shore was clear and well-trodden. They climbed a slight incline towards a copse of mixed woodland where curious squirrels sat and stared. As they had never been hunted for the pot, they had not yet learnt to avoid men.

The plateau on the rise gave a good all-round panoramic of the headland. To the south, in the middle distance, Easten clearly saw the outline of Birkenhead Priory. To the west, in the direction he must travel, there was nought but the sea between this point and Eire. He continued to turn. Somewhere to the north, though still unseen due to the dips and hillocks, was the settlement of mariners and boatbuilders he must hope would provide him the means of completing the next (and arguably most perilous) part of his mission, passage to Eire.

Easten turned again north, the direction he assumed

they would continue. Sure enough, just visible over the tops of the trees, he made out thin wisps of smoke from the cooking fires of a settlement.

Following his gaze, Roar nodded and grinned. "Hem!" he exclaimed, and with such fierce pride that even without the similarity of the sound he would have known Roar had just confirmed the location of his home.

The path meandered a gradual slope, through a young stand of pine forest. They reached a glade, identical to others they had travelled through. Roar paused and gave a cry that mimicked a woodland animal. Two young boys of about nine rose silently from one side of the path. With a minimum of gestures and fewer words, Roar sent them haring towards the settlement.

Easten felt Roar's hand on his shoulder. They had been walking side by side, but now his guide came around and stopped before him to look squarely in his eyes. The grin that had played on his face throughout their journey was replaced by a more serious look; what he had to say was evidently important.

He raised his open hand palm outwards and waited for Easten to do the same. Easten had seen similar gestures on his travels, indicating a lack of weapons and an offer of friendship. He had no hesitation in copying Roar's offer.

"*Ven!*" declared Roar, solemnly. Easten was astute enough to hear the similarity with the word "friend" and guessed that this (or similar) was what was intended by the gesture.

"*Ven!*" he echoed, gratified he had guessed correctly. The smile reappeared in Roar's eyes. With arms around each other's shoulders, they walked the final paces to the settlement as if they had known each other all their lives.

Several things happened all at once when they entered the ring of dwellings. A noisy stream could be heard chattering over a nearby stony bed, and there was a well-defined area of bare ground, smooth and free of grass, which formed a large, open meeting or assembly place. Everyone who lived in the settlement appeared to be there. Easten guessed there might be upwards of a hundred adults and almost as many children of varying ages; though none of the latter, he noted, were babes or toddlers. He took the opportunity to take stock, as he was unable to communicate with confidence and was obliged to rely on Roar for the first round of introductions and greetings.

Most of the assembled were much taller than Roar, approaching Easten's height but considerably heavier in build and weather tanned. They were naturally darker in complexion and favoured long, dark manes. Most of the adult males had long, well-brushed hair and beards, and some sported plaits and other decorations woven into them. They stood at ease, evidently listening carefully to what Roar said. As Roar paused, the person he had been addressing stood and opened his arms to Easten. He alone wore a head covering, which Easten guessed identified him as a chieftain or clan leader.

This he removed, placing it on his seat. "Erik," he rumbled, placing one enormous hand on his chest.

"Easten." He mimicked the action.

The first line of communication had been established, and Erik completed the open hand gesture followed by the hand clasp Roar had used on introducing himself.

CHAPTER FOUR

With stumbles—most cause for laughter rather than frustration—the remainder of the afternoon was spent patiently building a basic vocabulary. It was not long before Easten discovered that, for Nordic travellers to carry out even the simplest conversations, liberal quantities of liquid refreshments were required. One of the first words he learnt once they sat was "*Skaal*".

This, apparently, had to be said loudly every time a drink was taken. The drink was fermented, and therefore Easten presumed it to be alcoholic, but since it was neither wine nor mead, he had no way of guessing how potent. He determined he would restrict his intake to a socially acceptable minimum but found this difficult. After a while he felt certain his hosts were playing a game with him, to see how quickly they could drink him under the table. On the next occasion the drinks were poured, he placed a hand over his cup.

"*Nej... tak!* No." This had been easy enough to add to his vocabulary. For politeness' sake he had quickly established that "thank you" became "*tak*" but as far as he could tell there was no direct way to say "please", which struck him as odd.

There was a moment's silence, as if Easten had somehow committed a social gaffe. He looked at Erik and said: "V*i... praata.*" Then he made the same hand-caricature as Roar had earlier. Erik smiled and nodded. He drained his cup and stood. Those closest to him swiftly followed suit.

"*Ej flera pils!*" he declared, turning to Easten. "*Nej, tak… vi praata.*" He mimicked Easten's uncertain pronunciation but with no evident malice. Indeed, his tone hinted more at an approval that Easten would attempt to make himself understood with such little practice.

Erik indicated with a gesture that Easten should sit next to him, close to a convenient cooking fire. A pot simmered. Erik poured two warm drinks, then signalled to an older man who had risen along with everyone else and begun to follow them away to allow Erik and Easten privacy. As the newcomer came closer, Erik poured a third portion of the hot drink into the older man's personal cup, which he had carried with him. Cautiously, Easten sniffed it. It seemed not to be alcoholic: instead it smelt of certain herbs he recognised but could not name. It appeared an innocuous tea and tasted pleasant. Erik observed his reaction and roared once again with laughter.

"*Skaal!*" he thundered once more, drinking a substantial draught from his cup. With a wave of his hand, he indicated the newcomer should introduce himself.

The older man sat on a stool opposite Easten, placing his hand over his heart.

Easten noticed that he dispensed with the preliminary I-carry-no-weapon gesture: as a bard he was sensitive to such nuances, and wondered briefly what the explanation for this might be—if there was a reason.

Waiting until he had eye contact, Erik enunciated

clearly: "*Palle. Mig. Palle.*" Then, pointing at Easten: "*Du hedda Eee—sten.*"

Eastern caught the drift of the game immediately. "*Easten. Mig. Easten. Du hedda Palle…*"

Afternoon drew on, and the antiphonal two-way language lesson continued; Easten's skills as mimic and musician proved invaluable. Childish cartoon sketches drawn in the smooth clay and ashes around the fire site (and just as quickly erased) had also proved very useful. By the time an evening meal was served he had begun to string whole sentences together in an understandable manner. He was sure there would be time for a more formal 'fine tuning' of grammar later.

Early in their mutual teaching session, Easten established that Palle was also known as Stormsinger, and that traditionally Nordic voyagers such as these used two or more names, the second (and often subsequent) being a description of personal qualities, or possibly a reference to skill or function.

Palle Stormsinger was part-Bard, and therefore understood why Easten felt as he did about Perori's mystic qualities. He was also a skilled navigator. The name Stormsinger had been given him after he held the crew's courage in the face of a violent gale that hit them without warning during their voyage, and appeared to sing the storm into submission by force of will.

"So. You wish… sail west?"

Easten nodded.

"Yes. You sail… west… have sailed… Eire? Land?"

Easten felt annoyed at his lack of vocabulary, which prevented him asking clearly whether they knew of Eire or had sailed there before. Palle's face showed doubt, but he appeared to latch onto Easten's final word.

He crowed: "Land... west? Yes!" and signalled for Erik to join them.

Another sketch in the clay of the firepit. This was a recognisable picture of a rivermouth, which Easten assumed had to be the one they were in: after all, why would he want to draw another? A triangle mounted on a half-moon represented a boat—this symbol had been used several times during their 'lesson'. Three 'suns', which must stand for three days of travel, and a roughly oblong (or almost egg-shaped?) landmass to the west...

"*Baile Átha Cliath.*"

The words sounded strange in Palle's mouth, as if they were no more his language than one of those with which Easten was familiar. Seeing Easten's uncertainty, Palle added: "West men, name... not land... houses..."

An intuitive leap from Easten provided a possible term. "Town: house and house and house and..."

"Many house, houses: town," agreed Erik. Another important term had been added to their growing vocabulary.

Easten looked at the sketch again and pointed to the "suns".

"Sail Balley... three days?" He counted off three fingers of his left hand and mimed 'sleep'. Erik nodded once more, with a glance at Palle for confirmation.

Smiles on all sides. Easten had achieved something he had hardly dared wish for: a guaranteed passage to Ireland. He eased his tense shoulder muscles. Perori responded with a sweet chord, though he was unaware of consciously brushing his fingers over the strings. The chord grew and spread, rather than die away, rippling through the throng as they sat listening to the linguists attempting to understand each other. All conversation was stilled as the music flowed, almost like an invisible liquid, bathing them all with its soothing quality. Easten's fingers itched: the briefest of nods from Erik, and without even thinking about what he was going to play, and found himself singing. His fingers keyed the chords to a Welsh folktune, but the language was unimportant: his Norse listeners would not know the difference between Welsh, Latin and Saxon.

Nobody moved, nobody spoke; almost, it seemed as if nobody dared breathe for fear of missing the least nuance of the music shimmering over them—swirling, teasing and darting; hesitating, soaring, swooping unexpectedly to caress an individual ear before crashing on them all simultaneously. He reached the end of the melody and extemporised a series of variations. His listeners remained silent, some open-mouthed. Rather than fade and die, the final notes drifted among the canopy of the surrounding trees as if reluctant to depart. As the music spiralled starwards and soared beyond the limit of human hearing, the silence it replaced was absolute. The wild animals of the forest held their breath for an eternal moment: the leaves on the trees ceased their perpetual secret whispering as the faintest zephyr of a breeze died, leaving them motionless.

Easten stood, head bowed, waiting for a reaction. He felt emotionally drained. It was almost physical, as if he had just run until he reached his uttermost limit and somehow found the inner strength to carry on further.

When he thought about it later, Easten realised the time lapse between the end of the piece and the reaction of the listeners was in truth no more than seconds. As he waited, however, that space of two or three heartbeats stretched and filled as if time had opted to pause and lend an appreciative ear.

The spell was broken by the happy trill of a songbird, hidden deep within the treetops. Then came a deep, wordless sigh that coincided with the resumption of the breeze stirring life and movement back to the treetops.

Without a visible prompt Easten could spot, a deep-throated and rhythmic "Om—oom—oom" began from the audience spellbound at Easten's feet. As it grew in volume it was reinforced by the stomping of bootheels on the solid ground and the clash of tankards on tables, or hands slapping thighs. No words were spoken. Looking around, Easten could see from the clean-shaven men that everyone's lips were closed. They were humming, rather than speaking or singing and appeared to approve of what they had heard.

A young man about Easten's age rose, maybe in response to a signal Easten had failed to see from the leader Erik who was immediately behind him. He stopped steps in front of Easten, spread his arms, and dropped gracefully to both knees. Reaching behind his back he adjusted a strap that crossed his chest to reveal what Easten immediately recognised as a stringed musical instrument. This he laid at Easten's feet. Reaching into a pouch or bag on his belt he produced two more objects Easten did not recognise at once, but a flash of intuition led him to guess that they were more than likely other musical instruments. One thing he could be certain of: this was an offer of payment, in a gesture that could not be mistaken between cultures and communities who prized music anywhere in the world, without the benefits of a common language.

Easten looked to Erik. The Clan Leader nodded, smiled, and used his arms to indicate a 'giving' motion that removed any doubts. Easten took a slight step that brought him within touching distance of the giver of these gifts and placed one hand on his shoulder, encouraging him to rise to his feet. Embracing the young man (whom he—correctly—assumed to be the Chief's minstrel) he took the instrument carefully from the arms of the donor.

Hr then lowered himself to one knee and, without breaking eye contact, felt for and picked up the two smaller instruments which had been placed at his feet. Rising, he placed his arms around his fellow musician and embraced him once more, trying to make it look like the formal act of acceptance it represented in his own community and the court of his liege lord.

The subdued "Om—oom" chants that had now become significantly louder altered once more and became a well-orchestrated (but not musical) rhythmic chorus of "la-la-la."

"*Tak—tak—tak!*"

As he held all three objects above his head and nodded with a smile to acknowledge what he hoped was the crowd's approval, Easten wondered if he should just keep repeating this single word from the limited vocabulary he had gleaned. How many times, he wondered, ought he repeat the word to suggest the meaning of "Thank You Very Much" or something that corresponded to the phrase he himself would have used in his native Cymru to imply unfeigned gratitude? Was it already too late, he wondered.

And that was also a valid point; suppose repeating himself was only going to show him as an idiot, handicapped by that most dangerous of things, a little knowledge of any subject under discussion…

The musician stepped backwards and made a formal bow to Easten. When he unbent, he stood perhaps an inch or so over Easten. He was younger than he had first appeared. His pink, scrubbed skin showed no evidence of the need to shave either daily or even regularly. He made no attempt to address Easten but glanced off to the side where his Clan Chief still sat. Erik nodded and rose, planting a stave almost his own height and covered with intricate, detailed symbols and pictures between his feet. He looked directly at Easten and smiled. There was a wicked glint in his eyes, perhaps an inner private joke. He swept his staff diagonally across his body, mimicking a minstrel playing a lute.

He pointed first to the musician. "*Palle. Han heder Palle.*"

This was easy enough, compared with the intensive learning sessions Easten had already experienced. The musician's name was Palle, or "Pal—lur", stress on the first syllable: the spelling could be confirmed later, when Easten had cause to include the name in a ballad praising the young bard's skills. Erik slapped himself on the chest and continued: "P*alle… musik… mi.*"

Pretty obvious again, especially to a trained musician with an ear for the nuances of cadence in pronunciation of words in several languages. He noted the long "eye" of the final word and made a mental note to check the spelling of the personal pronoun, too.

Chief and minstrel stood and waited: the ball was now

in Easten's court, and some recognition or acknowledgement of understanding was required.

"*Tak.*" Hand on heart. "Easten." Nods from both men. So far, so good… With an exaggerated reverence, he held his own instrument at eye level. "Perori."

A soft murmur from the crowd greeted this pantomime. Doubt or puzzlement passed between Erik and Palle, and Easten sensed he had not managed to make himself clear. He tried again, scanning his limited Norse vocabulary.

"Mi—Easten." He raised the lute resting across his arms once more.

"*Mi heder Easten. Musik, heder Perori.*"

Palle reacted first, Erik a split-second later.

"*Namn! Jey heder Palle: du heder Easten. Luten heder Perori—ja?*"

"Yes!"

His fellow musician had made the connection, comparing the naming of people and the naming of an object, even something that did not possess the unique quality of a living, breathing, independent life of its own.

Erik spoke softly to Palle, a few words Easten could not hear other than as a rumble of consonants. Palle listened as if his life depended on carrying out a very specific task (which for all Easten knew of Norse mores might be the truth).

"*Pe—ro—ri spela mer?*"

On safer ground, Easten breathed a silent sigh. He was being asked to play again. This gave him the opportunity to try a more challenging piece and give a better sense of the instrument's individual capabilities.

He turned slightly to face Erik and bowed his thanks,

then settled Perori in the normal playing position on his shoulder strap. His fingers sounded a dramatic opening chord before he had the chance to make a conscious selection, and he found himself launched willy-nilly into a fearsomely complex melody, one of his own compositions written to honour his liege lord after a spectacularly successful staghunt. Faster and faster the notes tumbled from his flying fingers as he added the lyrics. He doubted anyone present understood them, other than himself, as the paean of praise was in the Welsh language, but Easten loved to sing. He possessed a surprisingly strong voice; his audience listened in silence, spellbound, though they understood not a word.

He had to concentrate as he came to a difficult passage but retained sufficient awareness of the world beyond the intimacy of his co-existence with Perori to sense that Palle had taken up his own instrument and begun to extemporise riffs and basic chords that complemented and filled out the melody shimmering between his fingers. This surprised him: despite his tender years, Palle was evidently a more than competent musician, and had found his way to the correct pitch of the melody without difficulty. Choosing and playing the correct sequence of chords without prior rehearsal was a skill that did not come easy, as Easten had found in his own early days and confirmed more recently when one or other of his apprentices had tried his patience with their error-strewn essays. He managed to listen with a critic's ear while concentrating on his own playing: as far as he was concerned, Palle was 'living' the music, performing faultlessly.

Easten began the final verse, building to the climax,

which told of the stag's capture and death. He caught and held Palle's gaze, willing his new acolyte to understand that they must end together with a final cadence: was that a glimmer of agreement in the young player's eye, he wondered. Apparently: for as Easten struck the final chord, sending a shower of brightly sparkling notes shooting into the foliage above, Palle contributed a vibrant chord that confirmed to all who heard that the epic tale had indeed reached its conclusion.

Palle nodded, perhaps in grateful acknowledgement for being 'allowed' to add an improvised accompaniment to the ode, or in recognition of Easten's skills.

Slowly he stretched out a hand, caressing Perori's smooth rosewood soundboard.

His lips moved as he murmured a word or two in hushed reverence; words that were full of respect and wonder. Perori's strings thrummed, though Easten was certain neither he nor Palle had touched them. A sweet cadence of notes pealed soft and clear, gentle yet audible, and hung undimmed, undying for impossibly long seconds.

"Beautiful." The word sang across Easten's conscious mind, though his eyes told him this was not the word Palle had uttered as his hand lay reverently on Perori's gleaming surface.

Easten was too stunned at this unexpected compliment. Whether it was referring to the music or instrument was unclear, but there was no mistaking that this was the word Easten heard inside his head, as clearly as if Palle shouted it. Yet he knew but a few words of Palle's tongue, and was certain Palle knew no Welsh… he was confused, unable to condense surprise into a question.

Palle's hand still rested on Perori, as if he were reluctant to break contact.

Easten aimed his right hand across Perori's silent strings and concentrated.

"How did you…"

Palle's eyes were large with wonder and apprehension, locked with Easten's.

"I… know not how."

"Nor I! But we are, somehow, hearing each other."

"Yes, Master!"

Neither of them had opened his lips during this brief interchange—of thoughts?—and there was no suggestion any of the bystanders and witnesses had been privy to their words.

"Take your hand from Perori. No, I am not cross, you do not offend her or myself! I simply wish to know if comprehension and the act of touching may be linked."

With reluctance (which Easten sensed), Palle obeyed.

"Do you hear me now?"

The blankness of Palle's eyes when he failed to respond told Easten all he needed to know. He had suspected this would be the case, but it had been necessary to carry out the test. Easten continued to lock Palle's gaze by force of will as he took the young lutenist's right hand and replaced it on Perori's belly.

"Do you hear me now?"

Palle resisted for a fraction of a second and attempted to pull his hand away with a look of alarm on his face.

"*Jai… hør!*"

Perori's strings trembled once more: this time more gently, discreetly, as if she had chosen to speak exclusively to the two musicians.

Easten 'heard' Palle's words as "I hear"—though the Norse and English phrases were not so different. He decided to press the young musician.

"Tell me what you hear me say now."

Palle hesitated. A puzzled look was swiftly replaced by inspiration. "*Fortæl, hvad du hører mig siger nu.*"

Easten was jubilant. He reached out and threw his arms around Palle's shoulders, embracing him in a crushing bearhug. "Perori has granted us the gift of tongues! She makes it possible for us to understand each other! Palle, you must explain this miracle to your leader, Erik…"

The onlookers, not being privy to Perori's private audience with the musicians, were aware that something significant had taken place. A low murmur of anticipation, even excitement rippled around the clearing as Palle relayed to Erik in a few well-chosen words the breakthrough they had achieved, thanks to Perori's unexpected but welcome assistance.

*

"Your… instrument, you say 'lyut', yes?"

Erik's pronunciation was close, but not perfect. Easten decided it was most diplomatic to accept the Chieftain's attempt at the name. He realised this was probably what he was accustomed to calling the instrument in his own language.

"Yes, lute. Our cultures are not far removed from each other, I think."

"Lute. Now, tell me again: how many times small (and not so small!) things have happened before today, while you have travelled with this marvellous instrument?"

Easten was at least prepared for this; he had a prepared answer he sincerely hoped would not sound prepared.

Easten and Palle sat at a round table with men selected by Erik to take part in discussions. The table was of a size that made it possible for any of them to place one hand on Perori where she lay on a rich velvet cushion in the centre while he spoke. By linking hands, everyone understood what the speaker had to say. Granted, the Norse colony had no language barrier between them (other than some small dialect variations), but to Easten it was a precious gift to be able to communicate quickly and without risk of being misunderstood—it would make his plea for assistance in passage to Eire immeasurably easier to achieve.

He rose to his feet and placed a hand on Perori's fingerboard. Erik and Palle each took hold of his cape, and around the table the remaining eight men linked hands. "During my journey through Cymru from Caradoc's manse I spent many nights alone, outdoors. On such nights, a traveller may be at risk of attack by wild animals: wolf, boar and others roam freely in the hills further south! Twice Perori alerted me to danger by chiming a strong discord, painful to my ears and on one occasion enough to drive off the attacker. When daylight came, I found the spoor of a large animal, possibly a bear. On the second occasion I was roused in time to defend myself: this wolfskin is my 'trophy'!"

He paused, producing the skin from his travel pack. As he held it above his head he could hear the murmurs of admiration from all sides.

"How can we use this magical weapon?" demanded

one of the men Erik had invited to the meeting. He sat directly opposite Easten, perhaps in his mid-thirties, and carried himself with the ease of a warrior.

Easten shook his head very slightly. "I do not think Perori can be used as a weapon. She is more a… a mediator, a bringer of Peace, healing, harmony…"

"At the very end of my journey north I was caught in the storm that blew last night. Perori could not hold back the storm: but I am certain I could never have found the sanctuary of the Priory without her guidance!"

"Why do you speak of this Perori as a woman?" another demanded.

"It's a beautiful instrument, I grant, but never a living being!"

"Amongst my people, it has always been the tradition to recognise the skill and craftsmanship of an object of beauty by treating it as if it were indeed a living, breathing entity," Easten replied. "Such powerful (and often magical) items are often referred to as having female personalities; probably because the Men who retell the ancient legends around campfires miss the female company they leave behind. There are many stories that have come down to us through our bards and storytellers which tell of healings, interventions and other small unexplained occurrences miraculous in nature. I am but a poor bearer of tales, not long out of my apprenticeship, and have not yet the skills to give me the right to rank myself as a true master of words, a *seanch'ai* entrusted with learning and retelling the history of the community I serve."

Erik lightly laid his bear's paw of a hand on Easten's shoulder. "You tell a good tale, poet! But if I had not witnessed…"

A gasp from behind and the resounding "crack!" of a wooden chair being overturned had Easten spinning on his heel in a defensive half-crouch. He was just as quickly put at his ease. The unexpected noise was not from a surprise attack, but Palle leaping to his feet and waving both hands as he addressed Erik.

"Your pardon for interrupting, Sire, but how can I be understanding every word you have just said to our honoured guest when neither of you are touching the lute?"

It was true, though neither had been fully conscious of it until it was pointed out. Easten glanced briefly at Palle, then back to where Erik maintained the lightest possible contact of fingertip on the crook of his elbow. Swiftly he formulated a sentence in his mind and took a breath to utter it when Erik reeled as if stung on his right palm by an angry wasp. He inspected his hand then banged it hard against his temple.

"What knavery is this? I hear your voice clearly in my head, saying that it's possible we no longer need to touch the lute to communicate, but your lips move not, and you yourself remain silent! How can this be?"

Easten struggled to maintain his inner composure. He felt dizzy for a moment. His 'inner ear' relayed Erik's words in the perfect, grammatically flawless Anglo-Saxon common to the sons of well-born families throughout the land, yet his eyes and the ears he had relied on all his life (until today) insisted the words issuing from Erik's mouth were not the sequence of sounds his inner ear was…

Interpreting? Was that possible? Could it be that looking after and caring for Perori over years was now being rewarded with an unlooked-for (but timely) gift, the understanding of languages?

From Erik's body language it was clear the Chief's patience (never one of his saving graces) wore thin. Easten had to find a convincing explanation, fast. He cleared his throat, trying for a grave manner of speech. "I personally believe the signs are thus," he began, stretching his staff in his right hand towards the fire a few feet from the table where the chiefs had opted to hold their meeting. Anyone who wished could observe the discussions, and almost everyone did. "Perhaps just being close to Perori is sufficient for the magic to work!"

As Easten spoke, Perori responded from the nest built for her honour and comfort, though none present had touched her. A pleasing chord rippled through her bass strings, growing in intensity, filling the air, lightening the hearts of all present. For no reason he could define, Easten was reminded of the loud purring of a cat with a full belly of fresh cream.

"It seems your travel companion agrees with what you tell us!"

An unmistakeable murmur of agreement from the audience accompanied by general nods told Easten that Erik was still speaking his own language while he himself 'heard' the English variation inside his head.

"This makes the request I now make far easier, but I have little to offer as payment."

Erik laughed. It was infectious: an unforced ripple of amusement spread through the assembly. "Poet, bard, minstrel, magician: whatever title you claim, you have already given my people and myself much pleasure with your music! A few more songs to entertain us through the long nights of winter could easily repay many favours! Come, drink with me in private, and we can discuss your urgent needs. I sense your throat is dry from the length of the lay you sang. Then you may speak freely; worry not on the favour you would ask!"

Erik turned and led off towards a half-timbered building, perhaps slightly larger than some of its neighbours, but not by much. Two young men in their late teens ran ahead and entered the house. As he approached Easten caught the unmistakeable sounds of bottles, glasses and beer tankards being rapidly laid out to await their arrival. By the time Erik had insisted Easten precede him into the dwelling, wine and beer had already been served at a small table in front of a cheerful, roaring blaze of sweet-smelling pine logs.

Taking his cue from the host, Easten picked up his beer tankard first. Erik raised his to his lips, pausing before taking a sip.

"Beer to ease a dry and dusty throat!" he chortled. "And *Skål!*—as we say when we drink with friends: the word means 'Your Health' or something like that. Do you have the same tradition?"

"I drink but little; it pays, in my liege lord's service, to always keep a clear head! But our customs are similar: 'Your Health' or 'Good Health' are probably the most common toasts I have used, and heard others use."

Erik roared with laughter once more; evidently, he was easily amused. He raised his tankard again, waiting for Easten to touch his against his host's before drinking, deeply this time. Easten followed suit. The ale was dark, with little foam. It was slightly sweeter than he was used to, but smooth and full of hoppy flavour. A voice warned him it was possibly potent, despite the innocuous taste.

Erik placed his empty tankard on the table between them and picked up the smaller glass. He inspected its contents thoughtfully, twirling the glass to the left and right, studying how the liquid moved rather sluggishly around the walls of the glass, as if slightly sticky.

He looked up at Easten: "This is a drink not all of your countrymen like. We take wine and 'burn' an extra time to make *brændevin*—'burnt wine'—also called by its Roman name in some parts when it is referred to as aqua vita, or akvavit. I hope you like it but have a care! It may be stronger than drinks you have tasted!"

Erik swallowed considerably more than half the contents of his glass and licked his lips. Forewarned by his host, Easten decided to sip at his and was pleasantly surprised at the smoky aniseed taste. A split second later he felt as if his throat was on fire, and he realised how important Erik's warning had been. Tears streamed unbidden from the outer corners of both eyes, but he managed to place the glass back on the table without spilling any of its contents.

"Drink loosens tongues."

Easten felt Erik's words sounded like an aphorism, and from what he'd heard of Norse habits and customs he suspected it was probably a translation. He was still vaguely aware that his host's lip movements didn't correspond to the sounds he was "hearing", but he was getting used to this; it no longer bothered him, though he still didn't understand how it could be happening.

Erik smiled, encouraging Easten to take the plunge.

"What I must ask of you I ask as a favour for another. My liege lord Caradoc, who is being threatened by a powerful, aggressive neighbour, has charged me to carry a plea for assistance to his brother in Erin. I must therefore beg for a swift sea passage to the west. Do you know of this land?"

"We have sailed many seas and beached on many shores since we left our homeland. Among them, we have indeed visited the land you call Erin. With a favourable wind, it lies about four days' sailing. The people are a hardy race: great warriors on land, but with little understanding of seafaring, or waging war at sea. I know not what they call themselves or their land, and we were not there long enough to set down roots, or name it in our own tongue…"

"And yet, we left some of our own there!" Palle added. He hadn't been included in Erik's invitation but tagged along anyway, in the same way as Easten invariably was normally never more than a few discreet paces from Lord Caradoc's side, acting as his personal aide in most things whether music was involved or not.

"My bard reminds me constantly of details of my responsibilities each day, and covers for me if my memory of events falters from time to time!" Erik sighed. "Yes, as usual, he's right! The battle we fought to carve a foothold on the eastern shore was fierce, and we were barely able to subdue them. Our victory was only assured when we stood offshore in our longboats and hurled rocks, fire and a rain of arrows onto their shoreline positions. Their shorter bows had not the power of our weapons, but it was a close-run contest!

"When they sued for peace rather than continue with a battle they could never win, and pointless loss of life on both sides, they proved trustworthy and observed the terms we demanded. They provided true hospitality and expert treatment for our wounded, who were treated no different than their own casualties. They even took many of our uninjured men who wished to visit wounded kin as they recovered, offering them bed and board in their private houses for as long as they wished. As a result, those too badly injured to continue the voyage opted to remain in the harbour town, Dubh Lyn—a name that in their tongue means 'Dark Water'—as did several of their close relatives who had perhaps tired of endless sea voyages and preferred to nurse their relatives to full health and settle there. The skill of the local healers was not to be doubted. I think we were about a dozen men shy of full crews on each longboat when we left?"

The question was directed at Palle, who thought for a moment before nodding.

"The beginnings of another Norse colony on a shore far from home," Erik said, and added with a certain glint of amusement in his eye, "Assuming they find comely wenches of childbearing age to put up with them. I wonder if that young woman I saw in your company on more than one occasion is still thinking of you?"

Palle flushed a shade of deep crimson but (perhaps wisely) resisted the temptation to rise to the bait.

Erik punched him gently on the arm to indicate there was no malice intended by the remark and turned his attention back to Easten. "So, in a word, you're asking me—at your lord's behest—for a passage to this land in the west which you name Erin. Is that correct?"

"That is the case, Sire…"

"Please! Until now it's been Erik and Easten; I'd prefer to continue that way."

"All the same that is my purpose in speaking to you today. I cannot offer a great deal in riches, jewels, or support for your own endeavours, my Lord Caradoc lives a considerable distance from here, and would be hard pressed to send help in reasonable time if you were in need of a few men at arms—but I know he would do so if you were to ask!"

"Tell me, Easten, are you a sailor?"

Easten was nonplussed. The question had no bearing on their discussion.

"We have rivers and lakes in Wales, but the region where my Lord lives is far inland, many leagues from the sea. Why does it matter?"

Erik's laughter rang out once more. "Only a land-crab could ask that question! Yet I hear no mockery in your voice; the question deserves a serious answer!

"Very well, then! Being on a ship, at the mercy of waves, tides, currents, and inclement weather is like no other existence, my friend! There are a hundred and one things you must have constantly on your mind to avoid being swept overboard while performing the simplest tasks, such as hauling on a rope to raise or lower a sail.

"If the cook manages to put a meal before you, you don't ask what's in it; you're just grateful it's there, and eat it without question. In many cases it's probably best if you don't know, anyway!

"Sleep when you can, where you can, if you can. You never know when (or if) you'll get another chance! I haven't even mentioned other seafarers yet, who are more likely than not to try to kill for the contents of the ship's hold, or even the very clothes in which you stand."

He paused, his frown resolved into a grin. "Still, I've

never known any other life and I wouldn't change it for a hold full of the most priceless treasures in the world! Every day brings a new challenge and I'm still the best at what I do, which is sail a ship.

"Your sense of duty to your liege lord is commendable, my friend."

Erik stood and snatched his glass from the table. With a blur (but without spilling a drop) his bear-paw of a hand passed over both glasses, filling them to the brim. "Of course I shall ensure you make safe passage to Erin! Only a churl would refuse! Also, I'll wait there at least a sevenday to hear from you in case you're obliged to leave in a hurry. I can't say fairer than that, can I?"

Perori's chord that greeted this remark was wild, full of joy and enthusiasm. Evidently it had also been heard (or sensed in another far more difficult to explain manner) all over the camp, even behind firmly closed doors, Easten heard muffled cheers and foot-stampings. For brief seconds bedlam ruled before pounding clogs announced the advent of a member of the community demanding the latest news, and an approximate departure time.

CHAPTER FIVE

"How quickly do you think you can ready a ship for the crossing?"

Easten found himself the guest of honour that same evening at a lavish *smorgasbord* feast. Ale and wines had flowed freely, and he felt he could ask the question without appearing impatient.

Erik took a long draught from his tankard before replying. "We always keep several of our longboats ready to launch. We feel more comfortable at sea! And if we find ourselves under attack, well, it's the fastest way to escape!"

"And those who will crew the ship, or ships, are they willing to risk the crossing?"

Erik blinked, puzzled. "My men will do what I tell them to do: that is the Viking way! And although the seas to the west can be difficult, we've sailed far worse over the years. I can tell you, this settlement on the banks of the Mørk Sø has been here for six, seven winters. For us, that's a long time and I sense that quite a few are beginning to feel restless, ready for new ventures. And here's a curious thing, the name the people of Erin have given the town where we left our injured men, Dubh Lyn, translates nearly as the same name we chose to describe this river, Mørk Sø. Both mean 'Dark Water'."

Easten glanced over his shoulder at the river flowing towards the last sunlight of the day. Though its lustre was reddish gold, it also carried a great deal of sediment from the riverbed, which lent it a dark, even 'dirty' tinge.

"I know my Lord Caradoc will honour without question any price you care to set for this venture…" Easten began. Erik shook his head, slamming his tankard on the table, perhaps a little more forcibly than intended. One or two of those closest looked around but Erik was still sober enough to wave them back to their own conversations.

"This is a matter of urgency for you, and you have explained persuasively the difficulties Lord Caradoc is *esp ek shper 'encing*…"

Erik paused and hiccupped. Easten nodded for him to continue.

"Honour has no price, and this warrior understands Lord Caradoc's needs, perhaps better than many would! He is fortunate to have a brother who is able to send help, and I am honoured to be of assistance! We have little use for precious metals, coin, or other tokens of wealth, but I will set a fair exchange of either goods or services, once we return!

"And you can make significant inroads on my bill for services to date by rousing your travel companion from her bed and persuading her to entertain us once more!"

Easten was secretly pleased to hear Erik refer to Perori as a female, rather than a lifeless wooden object, beautiful to look at, but without personality or soul. As he stripped back the layers of protective wrapping he whispered to her, "Come, Perori: this time we shall surely offer them an entertainment they will never forget!"

Easten played throughout the meal and received warm approval from the hundred or so rough (but not uncouth) warriors gathered for the feast. Had he accepted every cup of beer, mead or wine, he would never have stayed on his feet; he was grateful when Palle (who had shyly offered to accompany him after the first few ballads) relieved him from time to time with a solo number, some of which he played on a wind instrument carved from a reed Easten had never seen before. It produced a pleasant, whistling sound like birdsong.

Later, Palle produced another instrument, a skin stretched over a wooden frame he struck with a small stick to produce strong, exciting rhythms.

"I cannot say for sure what it's called," he admitted, when Easten expressed an interest, "I was given it as a keepsake, a memory, by a musician I met while we made repairs in Erin. Look, you can change the 'note' by squeezing on these two bars lashed beneath the skin…"

The cooking fires had burned low, the boar and venison which had been prepared over them now a happy memory, and the tables becoming bare of other foods when Erik lumbered to his feet. It was not necessary to call for order. Every conversation ceased as he rose, such was his authority. He raised his left hand and pointed east, where a constellation of three stars in a straight line had just become visible above the treetops.

"See, Brothers! Odin's Belt shows over our heads, pointing both east towards our own homeland, and west where we must set sail at first light!"

"Our new friend, this excellent musician, has urgent business that requires swift, safe passage to our last port of call before we arrived here and two of our fleetest longships will make the crossing. Those who have been chosen know who they are; they will also remain in harbour in Dubh Lyn and wait for him. Assuming his mission is successful, there will be extra vessels returning with you who may not know the way, and will need your guidance."

"Let us now ask Odin to protect us all in the coming days; those in the longboats, those who remain, and also the families and friends we left behind."

Erik faced the three shimmering stars of the constellation as they rose above the line of trees, gaining an extra intensity as they floated higher. As one, the rest of the Norsemen turned to honour the stars. A single note was sounded on a horn, and a hundred Norse voices chorused a stirring ode to their warrior king.

"Hail Odin, Battle Lord! We honour you tonight
Though far from home, we see your star so bright
Guide us as we sail on wild, uncharted salt foam
Grant us your courage, lead us safely home."

As the song ended Erik raised his tankard in a silent toast to the stars above: the rest of the company followed his lead.

"I will command one of the two longships that sail at first light. Easten and Perori will accompany me, and Palle will be included. He has shown skill with language that may be useful when we arrive. We cannot be certain Easten or Perori will be able to assist us. Get what sleep you can: both crews will need all their strength and endurance in the coming days!"

CHAPTER SIX

Easten was roused from the mountain of animal skins that served him as a bed for a few brief hours after the feast by a touch on his shoulder. In the flickering flame of a torch he made out a young boy who stood with a bowl in his hand. An appetising aroma suggested it contained something warm and edible. He propped himself on one elbow with as much dignity as he could and smiled at the lad, who seemed in awe of him and tacitly offered the food once more.

"*Tak!*" He was indeed grateful; not just for the meal but the fact that the simple word of thanks had been easy to learn, remember and pronounce. The boy's eyes flashed with pleasure. He bowed and backed out of the shelter.

The skins he'd slept under had not looked much like any bed Easten had slept in before, but they had certainly provided one of the warmest and most comfortable sleeping places, especially since the long days he'd been travelling. He sat up, looking in vain for a spoon before lifting the bowl to his lips and supping direct from the rim. His nose told him the contents were a boiled cereal, sweetened with crushed berries. Good travel food, he thought, solid and filling. He wondered how long it might be before he had another warm meal. How easy was it to cook meals on a Viking longship, at the mercy of unruly seas and uncertain weather? He shrugged, emptying the bowl rapidly. From what he'd understood it was a short crossing anyway, so perhaps meals were not a major concern. Packing was minimal. His only concern to ensure Perori was securely protected against the weather: he had few personal goods other than an extra cloak and change of shirt. He left the shelter carrying Perori and his clothing in one hand, the empty bowl in the other.

At once, Palle materialised. "You didn't need to bring the bowl with you!"

"It has to be washed before someone else uses it!"

"Maybe, but a guest isn't expected to perform such tasks. Someone who stays behind will do that. We are almost ready to sail! Come, I will help you find a comfortable berth for the crossing."

Palle took the bowl and placed it on a table outside the next house they passed on their way to a jetty where two vessels were being made ready. The first glimmer of dawn suggested itself behind a belt of trees on the opposite riverbank, where it bent around towards the east.

Erik stood next to the nearest longship. Other than the flag that fluttered from the foremast, it was identical to the second vessel in size and shape. In the uncertain light, Easten couldn't make out the design on the flag and assumed it was likely Erik's personal banner.

"Did you sleep well? And have you eaten?"

"Thank you, and yes to both questions!" Easten responded, shaking Erik's outstretched hand, grasping his elbow in imitation of the formal salute he'd seen used between the Norse men.

"Come, land-crab! Let me show you where to sit comfortably and in a place where you won't be in the way of my oarsmen!" Perori had remained silent throughout this conversation, wrapped in even more protective layers than Easten had used before, but Easten understood every word and had to assume that the same held true for Erik. Along with Palle he was led to a bench towards the stern of the ship where they were installed side by side. The bench was long enough for one to sleep on it, and there was sufficient headroom for the other to sleep beneath, with more than adequate space for their travel goods. They had barely taken their seats when a horn brayed, shattering the dawn stillness with a defiant blast. The sea eagle carved on the prow of the longship appeared to thrust out its chest, ready to defend the crew and passengers from any enemy foolish enough to deny their right to pass unchallenged. The sun cleared the tops of the trees as the river estuary widened and they reached open sea, casting a dramatically elongated shadow on the waves as the sails caught what favourable winds there were and made the task of the rower easier. A muffled drum and occasional snatches of rhythmic song helped the rowers establish a regular stroke. Soon Easten was certain that the prow must have risen. The ship cut cleanly through the water, suggesting it was meeting less resistance as her speed increased and she seemed to rise an inch or several.

"Perchance we'll fly to Erin!" he thought. This much, however, was certain: the contrary currents and unpredictable weather for which this quite narrow sea was famous—or infamous—seemed unlikely to slow their journey.

The bench he shared with Palle was set deep under the taff rail, giving them overhead protection against spray from waves striking the vessel's flanks.

"Have you ever sailed before?"

"No—unless you count my trip with your ferryman, Roar; that was an experience, I can tell you! But such a small, flimsy craft would never survive in these seas, surely?"

"You'd be surprised at how durable those small coracles are! We use them for fishing, and sometimes venture a mile or two offshore. These longships are built for speed and stability, for long voyages and as fighting vessels. They don't roll too much, so with luck you'll be spared the misery of seasickness. I hope you had a good portion of hot oatmeal this morning? Something solid in your stomach always helps!"

"Very enjoyable. Sweetened, I think, with some sort of berry, and honey?"

"Sounds as if we fed from the same pot! This is what we would reckon as a short trip, so we may not have the opportunity for another hot meal before we land in Erin, but we will be served hot drinks from time to time. Our meals—if you can call them that!—will likely be salt meat served on slices of rye, or other forms of… *håndmadder*— my apologies, I have no other word for this form of travel food!"

The term 'translated' in Easten's inner ear to "hand food" which sounded close enough to serve. Easten experimented with the 'feel' of the word in his mouth until he felt comfortable enough to add it to his rapidly expanding vocabulary of Norse terms.

He resumed his study of the rowers. Their muscles flexed and rippled beneath their leather jerkins as they pulled strongly on the oars, singing at the top of their voices to keep a steady rhythm. As a musician, he appreciated how the music helped. He glanced at the sails, noting how they strained at the masts.

"We have a good following wind," he remarked. "That must make their task much easier than if they were fighting against a blow from a direction other than the one we wish to travel."

Palle grinned ruefully. "Too true! I have indeed bent my back on the rowing bench when the weather has turned against us. It's not easy when the winds are contrary, but there are advantages in not being amongst the most heavily muscled on the crew, and Erik will only call on me (or others of modest build) when the ship is threatened, and every man is needed!"

Easten stood and stretched to ease his stiff muscles. Being a passenger had advantages, he admitted to himself, but sitting still for too long caused stiffness and cramps. From the vantage of his six foot-plus he had an unobstructed view to all sides. To his left—or south, he corrected himself—the green hills and valleys of his native Cymru were rapidly disappearing behind a rolling sea mist.

His eye was drawn to a dark mass close to the horizon a few points to the right of the prow—starboard, his pedantic thoughts amended. A cry from the rigging indicated the lookout had seen it, too. Erik thrust the tiller to a burly companion and bounced along the centreboard to the prow to get a closer look. Returning rapidly to his command position he spoke to two others, punctuating his remarks with gestures.

Easten turned to Palle. "What's happening? A stormcloud? Bad weather heading this way, perhaps?"

Palle frowned, then shrugged. He sniffed the air and shook his head.

"I smell no danger on the breeze, but we're losing the sails, so there must be something there he thinks we should be wary of."

Some of the crew, whom Easten judged to be still in their teens, were scrambling in the rigging loosening ropes, furling sail. The rowers changed their song and picked up the tempo of their stroke. Erik looked up as his discussion ended and strode purposefully toward them.

"Make sure your possessions—and especially your fine instrument!—are stowed as securely as possible. You might want to crawl under that bench and hold Perori in your arms. Whatever that is ahead of us, it's no stormcloud and at this distance too big to be another ship. But there's no land that I know of before we reach Erin—and unless I'm much mistaken, whatever it is appears to be on the move, and heading in our direction!"

Easten checked beneath the bench. Perori was stowed as securely as possible, padded between his minimal travelbag and Palle's luggage. He turned to Erik and shook his head.

"I am no sailor, but I am not a coward! I cannot tell whether what is approaching us is a threat, but I will face it on my own terms, and on my feet. If we must fight, so be it, but I will not run and hide!"

After the briefest of hesitations, Erik nodded. "May Odin fill you with the same *berserkergang* he sends my crew when they call on his name for battle!"

This time, the term Erik used didn't 'translate' inside Easten's head, but it was self-explanatory, and Easten had heard tales of how Norsemen threw themselves into battle, screaming and raging with fury as they swept all before them.

"One thing I must ask of you," Erik said soberly, "…and it is this. You must stay clear of the centreboard of the vessel if we are to fight at close quarters. You have not been trained in the tactics of battle in such a confined space!"

The sails had been furled and stowed before the conversation was over: the mast spars were bare. A curious construction of ropes, levers and a long, narrow wooden spar had been assembled near the ship's prow, and at intervals along both flanks of the vessel. When a pile of fair-sized boulders appeared behind each machine Easten realised it must be a weapon, the rocks were ammunition.

Palle noticed his interest. "*Slyngebøsse.*" Again, no translation offered itself. "It can heave rocks, fire and other weapons at an enemy from a great distance, far beyond the range of a lance or even the best archer. With it we can stand off the enemy and launch an attack without risking ourselves. From time to time we have even pulled back after a bloody hand-to-hand engagement and fired a salvo of the decapitated heads of our opponents. Until now, this has always resulted in surrender as our enemy sues for peace!"

A command must have been given, but Easten didn't hear it. Every rower stopped pulling, and every oar was raised simultaneously, dripping in perfect parallel Vs on either side of the longship. The hiss of her steady progress diminished as she lost way and slowed to an ungainly wallow on a sea that had become unnaturally calm, with no significant current or tide. Even the smallest wavetops smoothed into a flat, oily surface. Easten was aware that the wind had died; they were floating motionless on a dead stretch of open water, surrounded by an unearthly, somehow unhealthy silence.

The slap of a wave striking the vessel's flank near the prow was shockingly loud. Although it didn't exactly shudder from stem to stern, the ship rose just enough to be noticeable, starting from the prow as if a powerful wave was passing beneath her keel. Easten reached for the taff rail and clutched it tight.

Slightly to their right, at a distance Easten judged less than a halfmile from their becalmed position, a fountain of water erupted from the placid surface of the sea. It was followed immediately by the emergence of a hummock that grew swiftly to a hill and continued expanding until it resembled a mountain of mobile flesh dwarfing the longship, even at that distance.

"*Hvalfisk*!" Erik roared a command. Easten was confused, but the rowers were not. All along the port bank dropped their oars in the water and hung onto them but made no attempt to raise a stroke. Those on the opposite flank began a steady stroke, faster than any they had used so far. The ship turned from the position where the giant creature was emerging from the depths. It seemed oblivious of their presence; Easten sensed that, if it didn't alter course to attack in the hope of a tasty snack, it would pass them—just—on their starboard flank.

As the distance between the longship and the monster decreased, Erik decided the angle between them was sufficient and ordered the portside rowers to set to. They needed no second telling, as one they bent their backs and gave it all they had. The teen crews crouched over the starboard set of *slyngebøsse* released a salvo of rocks that fell close to the course of the approaching flesh mountain without striking it; Easten realised they were not trying to kill it, just persuade it to pass them by. He couldn't imagine them succeeding in killing anything of such a mind-numbing size, and prayed to every god this ploy would work. He dreaded the possible consequences if it didn't.

Although they were now picking up speed and (theoretically) had the vessel under control, the ripples from the passage of the great fish were enough to raise walls of water the size of stormwaves that came crashing on the ship, drenching everyone. Some loose items were swept overboard, lost. This was when everything hung in the balance. Had Erik's ruse worked? Was this monster of the deeps even aware of their presence, or would it decide to turn back and make a free lunch of them? Did such beasts 'think' in any sense of the word?

Several agonisingly slow seconds ticked by. Easten could hear his heart pounding; the increase in blood pressure made his temples sing, his ears thud.

The tension was enough to bring on a headache that clamped his forehead, threatening to cause him to choose between vomiting or fainting.

As he stood and fought for self-control, he realised the second wave to strike the longship caused far less wallowing and disturbance. A line of phosphor tracing the beast's passage confirmed what his eyes told him.

Fierce, battle-hardened warriors they might be, but the rough-and-ready crew of seasoned Viking seamen were apparently not worth the attention of such leviathans—or at least, not today, not just now anyway.

There was a ragged cheer from the deckhands, who stashed away the weapons just as quickly and efficiently as they had brought them out. With an economy of words and a few hand signals, Erik had them hopping to raise sail once more, and they continued to race away from their close encounter with disaster.

The winds continued to be in their favour. They made swift progress the rest of the day and had the open sea to themselves.

"How can Erik know where to head on an empty sea? There are no landmarks to guide us, and he said himself he has only sailed in this region once before, when you arrived on the banks of the Mersea from Erin?"

"He has led many successful *togts* over the years since we left our homes," said Palle, thoughtfully, "and so far we have always found a safe harbour when we needed one. The gods smile on him, I think. and perhaps his ability to steer a safe course is a gift of the gods too! My role as minstrel and storyteller means I am little more than baggage while at sea, so I have never learnt the mariner's skills, but I know he keeps a constant check on where the sun is in the heavens, and I believe that guides him when there are no familiar landmarks in sight."

Easten nodded. Land crab he might be but even he knew the sun rose and set in the same place each day. It was late evening and the dragon carved on the longship's prow stared with unblinking eye straight into the fiery orange-red orb as it prepared to sink beneath the waves.

"How big is the land we are aiming for? Is it possible we might fail to see it, pass too far to the north or south?"

Palle laid a reassuring hand on Easten's elbow and shook his head. "Erin, from what little I saw, is too large and solid a target to miss, especially for an experienced old salt such as Erik! I mean no disrespect, but I cannot express distances at sea in terms a land dweller might understand. How to explain…" He paused. "Before the daylight fails, look at the horizon—where sky and sea meet. Seafarers reckon the distance in leagues. The horizon we say is about eight leagues distant. At the speed we are travelling, that would probably take us about six hours in daylight, somewhat longer at night—but during the hours of darkness, Erik could use the stars to keep us on course!"

It was Easten's turn to nod. "Like you, I never had cause to learn how to navigate by sun or stars, though I know it can be done. But on land, you can also recognise towns, villages and other landmarks; here at sea, there are no roads to keep you from straying!"

The last light of the day faded, but there was still plenty of light provided by a full moon and the myriad stars that pulsated in a cloudless sky. Erik's silhouette was visible, standing tall at the tiller, gazing at the sky.

"When does he sleep?" Easten asked as Palle shook out several animal skins to serve as a warm nest for them to share.

Palle grinned. "I asked him once when we had been running before a storm for several days. His reply? I'll never forget: he told me, 'Sleep? Plenty of time for that when you die!'

"I'm sure it was an exaggeration, but he refused to let anyone 'spell' him at the helm until the storm had blown itself out!"

As far as Easten could judge, Erik was still in the same position when he was roused as dawn broke by a strident blast from a giant horn. Palle rolled out of his coverskins immediately.

"The alarm signal! Quickly, my friend, we may be

under attack!"

A vessel approached them rapidly and seemed determined to cut across their bows. "What makes you think they're attacking? They may simply be passing!"

"Basic rule, always assume another ship is a potential threat! That way you've a better chance of survival!" Palle responded as he burrowed deep beneath his belongings to unearth some of the ship's tackle also stored in their cubbyhole.

"Can you handle a sword, or bow? I can offer you a staff or cudgel, but if we get into hand-to-hand fighting we'll be boarded, fighting for our lives!"

"It's the law in England (and Cymru) that every man practice an hour every Sunday with the bow," Easten replied, "though I confess I've skived the last few weeks while I've been travelling—not that there was anybody to report my omissions to the local sheriff or landowner! I'm more than comfortable with a bow, thanks!" Palle handed him a bow and a quiver stuffed with arrows. Easten looked at it critically.

"Is something wrong?"

Easten shook his head. "Nooooooo, not really," he answered, "…but this style of bow is not one I have used often. Tell me what's the range of such a… small weapon? Can it measure up to our English longbow?"

Palle shrugged and nocked an arrow. He fired it high into the air, over the stern, and they watched it arc into the rising sun.

Easten held his breath and counted silently until he had a fair idea of where it would fall. "Hmm. Well, I didn't expect it to have the range of the longbow, but that's not too bad. As a tradeoff, I expect it's easier to draw… may I?

Thanks."

He tested the tension of the bowstring a few times. "Not bad. How accurate is it, I wonder? I suppose the only way I'll find out is by using it in battle… if there are enough archers on board, we may persuade them not to get too close!"

Erik had approached unnoticed while they were discussing the merits and demerits of the short recurve bow preferred by Norse seamen.

"We can all use a bow, though I grant you some are more skilled with this weapon than others!" he grunted. "But if you can suggest tactics which may improve our use of the bow, I'm always happy to learn something new!"

"Split the crew into at least three equal teams and form them up in staggered rows. If they shoot one row at a time you'll be firing an almost continuous volley, and the arrows won't collide or deflect in mid-air."

Erik's eyes gleamed with satisfaction. "An excellent idea; thank you, Master Tactician! If all the bards of England are as skilled in planning a battle as you, your warlords need have no fear of being defeated by any invader!" He strode off to issue appropriate commands, beginning with the striking of sails and the assembling of the clumsy looking but deadly efficient *slyngebøsse*.

"Let Erik lead off with the *slyngebøsse*, it's one of his favourite weapons!" Palle said, crouching back onto the benchseat, indicating Easten should join him. Easten sat, keeping out of the way as the rowers shipped oars and moved from the exposed rowing benches to gird themselves with sword and axe.

"It looks as if Erik has a surprise in store for them!"

Easten had been concentrating on the approaching

ship, close enough for him to determine it was a totally different shape to the longboat. He had been on the point of asking how Erik could identify the other vessel as a threat when it had been at least twice as far away, but the excitement in Palle's voice persuaded him to postpone the question, at least until Palle had the chance to complete his thought. He raised one eyebrow and encouraged Palle with a gesture.

"He isn't firing rocks, this time! Look, He's using dragonfire, which is much lighter and can be fired a much greater distance! In fact, our would-be attacker is about to find out the hard way why Erik Redhand always wins his battles!"

As Palle spoke, the *slyngebøsse* began firing. This time they didn't fire all at once but one after another in quick succession. Even if he hadn't been forewarned, Easten was sure he would have noticed that the ammunition was significantly lighter, as it rose higher into the morning sky before beginning its descent, arrowing with deadly accuracy directly towards the oncoming vessel and leaving a black, oily trail.

"Fire! When you mentioned 'dragonfire' I didn't realise you meant it literally! Of course, on a ship where there are so many things to be set ablaze, fire must be one of the weapons most feared—especially this far from land! No doubt they'll regret keeping their sails spread to gain the advantage of speed! Our archers may not be needed at all!"

Easten could see that the archers each had a deckhand at his shoulder carrying a torch. Staring hard at those closest to where he stood, he could just make out that they had strips of cloth wrapped around the head of their first arrow, nocked to fire. All that was required was to touch the arrowhead against the torch held by the assistant, and…

Before he could complete the thought, Erik must have given another silent signal Easten missed completely. The first salvo of burning arrows rose smoothly into the air. As the second round was fired, the first volley of blazing rags reached the oncoming doomed would-be pirate's position. Some landed harmlessly in the sea, but a high proportion hit either the wooden decking, or up in the rigging to blaze furiously, fanned into life by the ship's forward motion and almost impossible to reach or extinguish.

A ragged, poorly aimed volley was returned from the stricken vessel, but the longest of the shots landed harmlessly at least three or four ship's lengths short. The fire spread and the ship settled with frightening speed.

"We have them! They're going down!" Erik roared. The crew burst into a savage song, praising Odin for the ease of their victory, but Easten thought Erik seemed almost disappointed and mentioned this to Palle.

"Was he looking forward to a bloody, hand-to-hand scrap? Is that why he seems…" He paused, unsure of the best word to conclude his thought.

Palle glanced at the Leader for a moment, then shook his head. "He probably regrets the ship sank so fast before we had the opportunity to board and strip her of valuables they might have been carrying! All battles have their costs, and although we lost no men, the chance to scavenge plunder was lost!"

Easten stared over the expanse of sea once more. Some few remnants now bobbed and drifted on the surface, but the main hulk of the ship had disintegrated: whatever cargo her crew had was lost, irretrievable even in the relatively shallow seas between England and Erin.

"Should we sail in and seek survivors?"

Palle had a look of incredulity on his face. His eyebrows disappeared into his thick unruly blond hairline. "You mean, rescue an enemy? Save the lives of those who tried to murder us? Go short on rations to feed extra mouths? Is that how the English wage war?"

"You mean, you'd leave them to die from drowning or starvation? Is that how a brave Viking hero shows respect for a vanquished foe?" Easten retorted.

Erik approached, and one glance was enough for him to sense the tension, the struggle of wills. "Ho! What gives cause for this discord between two of the finest musicians I know?"

Both began to repeat their opinions of the whats and whys of the situation, neither prepared to be the one to back down and allow the other to speak unimpeded.

After a few seconds, Erik roared, "Enough! Must I command you to speak one at a time? I have two ears I grant you, but I cannot judge right or wrong if you insist on shouting each other down!" Both musicians looked shamefaced. Erik nodded. "Good! Palle, since you are my responsibility and I have had the dubious privilege of knowing you for many years, perhaps you might care to speak first?" Visibly chastened, both gave their views in a few brief words. Erik gave no sign of approval or rejection of either argument but stood and chewed absently on his moustache before he turned to Easten.

"Palle is right, of course. It has never been the Norse way to take hostages after a battle. We believe if you save a man's life, you are responsible for his welfare, at least until he is once more able to take care of his own fortunes. And the point he makes about feeding extra mouths while we are at sea is a good, practical reason not to delay our mission by searching for possible survivors."

He turned his attention to Palle. "You have been at my side for a number of years and shown skill with words of advice as well as entertaining us with your musical gifts. And on more than one occasion you have persuaded me to temper justice with mercy, when the lust of battle was still on me after a victory, and I was more interested in taking revenge for the death of fallen comrades!

"But we are men, not mindless animals! There are times when we must take new ideas from others we meet. Easten has suggested we look for survivors instead of leaving them to a lingering death by drowning. That is surely something a hero should be proud to do!

"We will follow Easten's suggestion and look for survivors. We must be swift; they will not last long in these cold waters!"

The rowers bent their backs to the oars once more and the sails were trimmed to take advantage of what wind there was. The longboat skimmed across the waves to the flotsam and jetsam that marked where the enemy ship had gone down.

As they approached, the rowers raised their oars; sails were trimmed further and they slowed to inspect what they were floating past. A few barrels and broken masts could be seen, bodies draped across them, clearly past assistance.

"There is one here, waving!" Palle cried, pointing. He had his jerkin off in a flash, before anyone could stop him, he snatched the loose end of a coiled rope and flung himself over the side, forging through the chop of wavelets towards the survivor. He passed the rope under the man's armpits, turned onto his back and sculled back to the ship, cradling the wounded man's head on his chest. Willing hands heaving on the other end of the rope made the return journey easier than the outleg.

Getting the victim onto the ship wasn't the easiest part of the rescue, but they managed it. The victim made it easier by passing out from the pain of jarring his broken leg against the flank of the ship as he was being manhandled over the gunwale.

"Get splints and lengths of wood: staves from a broken barrel would be ideal! And a fur for Palle, before he freezes!"

It was Easten's turn to make himself useful: he rolled back his sleeves and signalled for the unconscious stranger to be laid out on the nearest flat surface, the top of a large chest near Erik's command point.

"Warm water—not too hot!—to clean his cuts and minor wounds," he ordered, tearing a piece of cloth into narrow strips. "I need to straighten his leg while he is in a swoon. I fear the pain will most likely awaken him but that cannot be helped!"

Three or four pieces of wood appeared, each with the distinctive slight curve that identified them as having once been the staves of a barrel. With a murmured thanks Easten chose two and lashed them to the damaged leg.

"Someone hold his head; put something solid in his mouth, to prevent him choking on his tongue!"

Working swiftly and carefully, Easten straightened the injured leg and bound it as tightly as he dared, listening for signs the patient was feeling a level of pain that threatened to rouse him from the convenient state of merciful oblivion. He breathed relief as he tied the final knot, aware of a surrounding silence. Not one of the dozen or more people standing within an arm's reach of his improvised *chirugeon's* table had spoken throughout the procedure, and none were prepared to now he was finished. He looked round, confused. Had he broken an unspoken rule, taking command of a shipboard situation without permission?

"Why do you all stare, yet say nothing? Am I wrong to treat this man's injuries? Have I offended some warrior code of yours?"

Erik stepped forward. "They wait for my judgement in this, my friend of many talents! That is our way and generally it serves us well." He placed an arm around Easten's shoulders and hugged him close. "The giving of orders is something my men expect to come from me: not from another, even one with a talent for doctoring, apparently, in addition to the skills we have already seen you display!"

He paused, then raised his voice to address the whole crew. "Our friend Easten has shown today a new and useful talent, and I am pleased he had the courage to take command, possibly saving the life of a total stranger. His ways are not ours, but that doesn't mean they are less noble, less heroic! Now, continue to search for any other survivors while we find a comfortable berth for the injured man!"

The victim moaned and showed signs of awakening. The crew returned to gazing out over the detritus which bobbed around them. An occasional splash indicated that someone had taken the plunge to make a closer inspection. The injured man was made as comfortable as possible on the bench Easten and Pale had slept on overnight. By now the pain in his leg had completed the waking process, and he moaned softly, mumbling in a language none present understood.

"Do you recognise his words, Master of Languages and other skills?" Erik's question might have been laced with amusement, but there was neither venom nor mockery. Easten shook his head and studied the sufferer more closely. Returning consciousness inevitably made him more aware of his injuries and he began to writhe, agony writ large on his features. He gestured to two burly rowers to steady the patient, immobilising his shoulders and hips to prevent him making his injuries worse.

"He wears a cross on a chain: we can assume he is of the Christian faith."

Easten murmured. "There is some sort of badge or design on his jerkin: possibly part of a uniform? Small in stature and darker in skin than one from any of the Angles, Saxons or Celts I have met on my travels. Their ship appeared to come at us from a southerly direction. Could he be from Normandy or Gaul? It's not too far—closer than your homeland, certainly!" He gently smiled at Erik.

The patient was now almost fully conscious. When his eyes snapped open, they were a deep, muddy brown; not the clear blue common in Celtic tribes and Norse seamen.

"Gaul, Normandy, Iberia… some southern clime where the skin is darkened by hotter summers than ours, you think? There may be truth in that," Erik remarked.

Easten enjoyed the chance to use his powers of observation, but had to remind himself it was most definitely not a harmless game intended to entertain or pass an idle hour. It could have great importance, depending on what they could learn from their efforts, and they had to be certain whatever information they deduced was accurate.

Easten signalled to the rower holding the patient's shoulders to help him to a sitting position. Locking the stranger's eyes with his own, Easten poured water into a drinking horn and deliberately sipped before passing it over with what he hoped would be understood as a smile of encouragement.

The patient needed no second bidding but emptied the draught gratefully and held out the empty horn, clearly asking for a refill.

"*Agua.*"

"*Agua.* Water," Easten replied as he refilled the horn. He made a connection, something he'd always known without remembering where or when he'd heard it. He turned to speak directly to Erik. "This could be important; for hundreds of years, there was a common language throughout most of the countries south of these Isles, at first due to the all-embracing Roman Empire, later carried on by the presence of the Christian church. It was the native tongue of the all-conquering Romans, of course: Latin!"

"And you have already shown us that your Perori can assist us with understanding a language!" Palle interrupted. "…I could even understand the words of the Ave you sang during our feastmeal: that was Latin, was it not?"

Easten agreed that the Ave Maria Palle was referring to was indeed in the Latin language. In the absence of a better suggestion, there was nothing to be lost by trying…

Perori was carefully, almost ceremoniously, extracted from her layers of protective covering and laid on a soft animal skin between Easten and Palle, side by side close to the patient's shoulder. Both musicians reached out and laid one hand on the lute. The stranger looked puzzled, then stretched out a trembling hand, hesitating and looking for a nod from Easten before committing his hand to Perori's belly.

"Water… *Agua*."

"*Agua*… Water."

The Litany progressed, building up a vocabulary of basic words to establish a rudimentary understanding and make essential dialogue possible. Having been through a similar situation in the Norse settlement on the banks of the Mersea river, Easten achieved this task far more quickly and efficiently.

"*Dormibus* … We will sleep."

Easten stood and stretched. He'd been concentrating so hard and for so long to establish a linguistic bridge, he hadn't been aware of the passage of time or even his cramped position next to the locker that served as the makeshift doctor's office, sickbed and interrogation chamber.

CHAPTER SEVEN

The longship crossed and re-crossed the area of sea littered with wreckage, but no more survivors were found.

"We have our own mission to complete; time to raise all sail and continue west," Erik said, and turned to bawl a string of orders to the younger crew members, the 'rigging monkeys'.

Easten had gained enough of the survivor's trust to learn that his name was Anton. Inner warmth in the form of heated wine, and outer warmth provided by a heavy animal pelt had cemented this trust, and Anton drifted back into a healing slumber, temporarily freed from pain.

"Will he recover?"

For all his size, Erik could move as silent as a cat. Easten hadn't noticed him approach and started in surprise.

"His leg will probably cause him discomfort, but he seems fit and healthy. The signs are good, I think."

"Where did you learn how to treat war wounded?"

"My master Lord Caradoc has powerful neighbours; that, after all, is the main reason I asked for passage to Erin! He has had to fight many skirmishes, and we who live under his protection have had to learn skills and play our part when necessary. I have not the strength and stature to be an effective warrior, so I learnt to dress wounds and heal the injured."

"I think you are too modest; healing the wounded is a skill that deserves greater recognition!"

Easten shrugged. "We must all do what we can… have we lost much time while searching for survivors? How far are we from reaching Erin?"

Erik threw his head back and surveyed the starscape overhead. "Our bearing is exactly as I would wish. I expect to see Erin's coastline clearly by sunrise."

"Really?" It was Easten's turn to be surprised.

Erik nodded confidently. "We may not have sailed these waters frequently, but I know them well enough to be sure of that. The harbour at Dubh Lyn is easy enough to find, and we will be well received when we arrive. I suggest you try and get some rest yourself. I notice you and Palle have handed your assigned sleeping place to our… extra passenger. That was a noble deed, and you should not suffer for your thoughtfulness!"

He took Easten's elbow with one hand and Palle's with the other. Striding purposefully to the prow of the longship, he cuffed several rig monkeys from the lea of a piece of deck furniture where they had been crouching and installed the two musicians there instead. A growl produced a selection of furs to be used for comfort and warmth through the remainder of the night. Easten was asleep almost before his head landed on the furs.

It wasn't the raucous cry of a longhorn that roused Easten, nor a rough, well-meant shake of his shoulder. A large, arrogant gull perched on the gunwale above his head and uttered a second ear-splitting shriek of defiance as he opened his eyes and focussed on it. He lunged at the unwelcome scavenger: like every bully, beneath the bluster it was a coward and shot off for an easier target. A giant rower towered over him and pointed the way the gull had taken.

"Land!"

The term needed no translation: the Norse was close enough to the burgeoning English language. Easten scrambled to his feet and screwed his eyes half closed against the dazzle of the low morning sun. Off the port bow, every wave was transformed into a thousand diamond needles, impossible to look at comfortably as they magnified the rising sun's rays.

Closer than he'd thought possible after two days sailing, a low rugged coastline filled the horizon. They were close enough to see bays, headlands and the green of hills and fields sweeping close to the shoreline. Easten remembered what he'd been told the previous evening about judging distances at sea: they had to be no more than two or three miles from land, but they were still too far to make out finer details to indicate a town, or even smoke from fires or another vessel. Palle stood at his side, gazing at the landmass.

"Will Erik be able to guide us to the harbour you spoke of? You told me you'd only been there once, and I see no sign of a human presence."

"If you knew anything of our history or our seamanship, my friend, you would not need to ask such questions! Can Erik find a harbour—any harbour—anywhere in the known world? That's like asking if a man needs a daily reminder of how to breathe, or if a bear shits in the woods!"

The unexpected crudity made Easten smile. Palle grinned. "Our detour on the mission of mercy you persuaded us to carry out means we are approaching Erin from a more southerly direction than planned, but all we need do is sail north, with the coast on our left, and we cannot fail to reach Dubh Lyn sooner or later. Remember, Erik expected the crossing to take three days, and we have barely been at sea for two. I am no navigator, but I expect us to reach our destination today. The gull was the first clue: they never stray far offshore!"

"We'll make port within the hour."

Once again, Erik had arrived unnoticed. He spoke to Easten and Palle, but the focus of his attention was on the shoreline off the port quarter, appreciably closer even in the past few minutes. As he peered into the mid-distance Erik stiffened, raised his head, and sniffed the air. For no logical reason, Easten did the same, but to no avail; he sensed no change whatsoever.

"What do you… sense, smell…"

"The breeze at dawn is always offshore, wherever in the world!" Erik replied. "There is just enough 'carry' for me to taste the woodsmoke of a fire. Heating or cooking, it makes little difference. It's a sure sign of a town of some size close by." As the longship reached and passed the next promontory, a large, busy harbour spread before them. Craft of a variety of shapes and sizes skimmed back and forth. There was the unmistakeable aroma of smoke, fish, wet sisal and fermenting, gently rotted seaweed typical of ports and harbours.

The smaller craft scattered like minnows before a pike as the rowers shipped oar to avoid swamping them or causing injury to their occupants. The sails were trimmed to reduce their speed as they drew nearer to the quayside; a medium-sized vessel with a large flag on its main mast detached from a jetty close by and headed directly towards them.

"I recognise the emblem. It's the Harbour Master's flag. He will guide us to a vacant mooring."

Erik waved to the approaching craft, taking the tiller to perform the final, delicate docking manoevres. Under his confident handling, the longship nestled against the quayside, a serene swan returning to her nest. Once mooring ropes were secured fore and aft, the Harbour Master was waiting patiently to board.

Erik caught Easten's eye. "When we left here, it was with smiles and good will, but we were still at the stage of guessing what each was trying to say to the other; our discussions were still more hand signs and mime than speech! I think it might be an advantage if your unique musical instrument could mediate?"

"We'd be honoured to help in any way!" Easten assured, "and I suggest Palle joins us. He tells me he managed to acquire a few words of their language in the short time he was here. I believe he made friends among their people, too."

The three-man delegation signalled to the Harbour Master they would join him on the quay rather than expect him to scramble on the longship up a rope ladder.

"Apart from anything else, this is more practical. As you may have noticed, there is neither cabin nor private quarters on this vessel, and there are matters best discussed in private."

Mime and hand gestures sufficed to relay a request for private audience to the port official, who led them to a small building at the end of the jetty. Two other men remained in the room with the Harbour Master, but the main room was surprisingly spacious and didn't feel overcrowded. Erik gestured for Easten and Palle to stand either side of him at a table, the main piece of furnishing. Once the door was secured, the Harbour Master stood opposite Erik with his assistants balancing Easten and Palle. With a gracious nod, he indicated they should all take their seats. Glasses and a bottle materialised; the Harbour Master raised his glass in silent toast, draining it in a single swallow. Erik looked swiftly left and right to ensure Palle and Easten understood the moment's significance before emptying his glass in the same fashion.

Easten had assumed the contents were a form of alcohol, but the potency of the drink and the manner it scalded his throat took him by surprise. He caught an unguarded half-smile on all three of the faces across the table but when none of them coughed, gasped, or gagged this was replaced by a more serious look of... respect? Genuine, frank smiles followed as the glasses were refilled, and an open palm gave Erik (he hoped) the opportunity to open the discussion.

At Erik's nod, Easten stripped away the layers of Perori's protective valise. In silence, he laid her in the centre of the table. The representatives of Dubh Lyn's harbour watched. They evidently recognised Perori as a musical instrument, but the doubt in all eyes was unmistakeable; clearly, they could not guess why Erik had introduced this item, though it was clearly an object of outstanding beauty. "May the gods smile on us now!" Erik murmured as he stretched his hand and laid it on Perori's belly. Easten offered a silent prayer with the same plea (though framed in a different language). Belatedly, he realised any demonstration of the linguistic gifts Perori made possible required him to speak. He nodded to Erik and turned his attention to their hosts. He reached across the table and took the harbour master's hand, placing it on Perori, close to his own and Erik's but not touching either. This was the moment: would the magic work once more?

"We thank you for welcoming us to Dubh Lyn, and the captain of our vessel, Erik, has asked me to say he is also grateful you have honoured your promise that we would be received as friends."

He stared into Harbour Master's eyes for the least sign. Comprehension, revulsion, shock, horror; any reaction would be better than nothing…

An invisible hand caressed Perori's strings or at least that was how it seemed to Easten, who could see clearly none of the three hands barely touching the instrument had plucked at them. All the same, he wasn't prepared for their host's unfeigned reaction: amazement and wonder, relief and joy. As before, the evidence of his eyes told him the words the Harbour Master's lips formed were not the words sounding in his mind but knew he understood the speaker perfectly.

"I know not how 'tis possible, but your words are as clear to me as if we had lived in the same village the whole of our lives! How can this be?"

"We cannot explain it; indeed, we only discovered by chance that this wondrous instrument makes it possible to understand a speaker's words."

"You bear a cross at your throat, symbol of the new religion brought to Erin by Padraig and Brendan, so you are not a sorcerer, dealing in the Dark Arts?"

"No, that I promise! My name is Easten, and I was born in Cymru…"

With a minimum of words he introduced himself but made no mention of his journey's purpose. He was conscious of the bafflement on the faces of the two as-yet unnamed members of the group and sought to include them.

"Ask your friends if they have understood anything we have said so far."

As the Harbour Master turned to question his aides, his hand momentarily broke contact with Perori's surface. As swiftly as the snuffing of a candle, the contact between them was broken. Easten heard the words of an unknown language as the Harbour Master questioned his colleagues, and the negative headshaking from each confirmed his suspicions.

"If you now ask them to place their hands on Perori, as we do—or even touch your cloak, or your shoulder—I think that will suffice to grant them the understanding of our speech in the same manner as you experienced it."

The expressions of amazement on the faces of the Harbour Master's assistants confirmed what Easten guessed, and a full hour sped by with a bewildering amount of information passed between full grown men from three different lands, each speaking his own native tongue yet able to understand what was being said by the others. The only common factor was the intervention of Perori, whose strings hummed softly from time to time, whether a hand was laid on her or not. Easten was never certain, either that day or in the days that followed when he had time to reflect on the meeting, at what point they had advanced from needing physical contact with the lute to understand each other's speech to a state of being able to communicate without assistance. He recalled how rapidly the change had taken place back in Erik's settlement in Leverpole, so why should he be surprised when the same minor miracle was achieved again, involving a significantly smaller number of minds?

The Scripture parable about the gift of languages coming to the first Apostles, granting them the ability to speak in many tongues surfaced in Easten's mind, from early studies of the New Religion he had followed before being baptised into his chosen faith. For a moment he felt uncomfortable. Was it sinful pride to compare this with God's gift to those He was sending forth to proclaim the Gospel, the Good News? That, he decided, was something to lay away and debate with himself (or possibly with a priest who might advise him) on some more appropriate occasion.

Personal introductions were the first formalities. The Harbour Master's name was Simon. Easten was glad to 'hear' a name that sounded familiar; he decided to assume the spelling used for the first among the Twelve disciples. Simon's aides were introduced as Peder and Leon. The latter was indeed "crowned" with a lion-like mane of thick, wavy blonde hair, which made it easier for Easten to remember which of them he addressed: they were clearly siblings and (hairstyles apart) had similar features.

The torrent of information flowing back and forth made thirsty work of their discussions, and before long several bottles lay empty around the table as they all had a tale to tell or a question that needed answering. It was only when the sun moved from the window and the light in the room faded that they became aware how long their first contact meeting had become.

Simon turned and spoke a few words to Peder, who

nodded and left the room.

"He will soon return, he's gone to make sure we are fed!" Simon said with a smile. "Long discussions are first and foremost thirsty work, but we should remember to soak up the liquid with something more solid!"

Until food was mentioned, Easten hadn't realised how hungry he was. They hadn't bothered eating before leaving the longboat early that morning, and his stomach growled so loudly that he looked around, embarrassed at the thought it must have been audible to everyone.

Erik caught his eye.

"Relax, friend! Your belly is not the clatter-tail you suspect! But it may become necessary for us to find ways of shielding our innermost thoughts occasionally, for I read you as easily as an open scroll! We are all as hungry, I think, and ready to break bread with our hosts! We have achieved much today, in large part thanks to the unique gift supplied by the instrument you name Perori and insist that you think of as 'her', as a travel companion rather than a 'possession'. Would you consent to play, entertain us while we wait for food? Our hosts have not yet had the pleasure of listening to the sweet music 'she' can produce!"

Easten needed no second bidding, turning and reverentially lifting Perori from the place of honour she had occupied in the centre of the table. As had happened with increasing frequency during the past sevenday, his fingers knew exactly what music would suit the occasion.

He closed his eyes and relaxed, trusting his fingers to seek the correct stops on the fingerboard. At once, ripples and cascades of living, breathing music flooded from Perori's depths, as if they had been imprisoned in her belly forever and would no longer be denied their freedom. The melody was triumphal: the music skittered across the room; so lively Easten was convinced he could see the notes taking physical form, dancing freely, tantalisingly close to visibility.

The room felt too small to contain the music as well as the human occupants: Easten was not surprised when the window burst open, though none of them were close enough to release the fastenings. A crowd was already gathering outside, many open-mouthed, listening in silence.

The music ended with a joyous shout of a final cadence. Easten damped the final quivering of Perori's strings, using the palm of his hand to caress her with the gentlest touches. For seconds nobody moved even appeared to draw breath.

The spell was broken when a door opened, off to the left. Two young girls stepped out, carrying loaded platters: they stopped and gazed at the silent crowd, then scurried across the docks to the Harbour office.

"Our refreshments," Simon murmured. "However, we seem to have drawn the attention of several people! Would you be willing to introduce yourselves—and your musical companion!—to the community, over a shared evening meal?"

Easten looked at Erik, who said, "My authority is over my community, and vessel; I am as much of a foreign guest here as you, my friend, but you are the man with a mission still ahead of you and who understands this marvel best. The next move is yours!"

Easten turned and nodded to Simon, not trusting himself to speak. Simon strode to the fore and relayed the invitation to all present.

"Once we have seated ourselves and brought forth refreshments, our guest has promised to explain for us the magical powers of his musical instrument—which, as I'm sure you've already realised, are very real!"

A cheer reverberated from surrounding trees as the audience dissolved into a flurry of purposeful movement. Benches, seats, and covered dishes appeared in short order: kegs and bottles of various sizes and shapes threatened for a short time to outnumber the dishes of food, but once everyone had returned with their contribution to the impromptu feast the balance was somewhat restored, though the trestles had begun to sag dangerously under the weight. Three tables were placed together immediately outside the door of the house Easten had to assume was Simon's "office". The two girls who had unwittingly broken the tableau by emerging with covered platters placed them on a snow-white sheet, elevating the status of this to a 'Top Table' and confirming that Easten, Palle, Erik and the Harbourmaster's delegation were the 'honour guests'.

Easten drew Simon aside as the Community gathered and took their seats. "You may think this request... odd, but it would please me if Perori could be 'honoured' with a seat at the table. As I told you, to me she is my companion on the road, not just a wonderfully crafted, beautiful instrument. Since our understanding of each other would not have been possible without her assistance, it seems only right everyone present should be aware of this."

Simon called someone to his side, who listened without comment, nodded and sped off. "I have asked one of the village musicians to bring a suitable seat, and another... I am no musician, I don't know what it's called, or even if it has a name! But I know our musicians use it to stand their instruments safely between sets, when they play, and I think it will fit easily on Perori's seat at the table and make it easier for everyone present to see her."

Easten was gratified to hear Simon refer to Perori as "her" rather than "it". Perhaps a minor matter, but to him it suggested his task to convince the local community of Perori's unique nature and powers would be easier.

Before they sat to begin the meal, Simon signalled to someone Easten couldn't see, on the far side of the square of open ground where the long table had been set up and filled from end to end with food and drink.

A young man stepped from the lengthening early evening shadows of the trees, carrying a musical instrument of some sort and lending an elbow in support of an elderly man with long, pure white hair who was dressed in a robe covered with embroidered designs, clearly a badge of office. They advanced without haste but with due ceremony and paused before the Top Table. Simon bowed deeply and made the introductions.

"Easten, I have the honour to present for you the wisest man I have met, our *seanch'ai*, Turlough. He is our storyteller, our poet, our teacher, and knows all which is to be known of our history. He is often called on to make judgements in disputes, and I sense we may be calling on all his experience and wisdom before we sleep."

"I am honoured to meet you, My Lord,"

Easten bowed as he greeted the elderly man, bending just far enough to make it possible to maintain eye contact. The surprise in the sharp eyes of the older man was all he needed to confirm that Turlough had heard and understood his greeting but was at a loss to understand how. He offered the *seanch'ai* his hand and added, "Please do not be alarmed; I promise there is neither sorcery nor spells at work! One of the reasons for this festive meal was to grant me the opportunity to explain as best I can that Perori—who for me ought to be the main honour guest this evening!—has somehow granted us the gift of understanding. I believe this has been achieved through the power of music, but confess little understanding of how this is possible."

"Easten. Perori." The *seanch'ai* seemed to be tasting the names as if it were possible to thereby learn something about both of them. At once he realised that this should not be dismissed out of hand. It was an undeniable fact Perori had made possible an instant understanding and dialogue between people of at least three cultures, backgrounds, and languages. This should have been unlikely (if possible), yet it had happened. If the community wise man felt this was the 'right' way to deal with new knowledge, it was not Easten's place to doubt him.

Satisfied that he had learnt the correct pronunciation of the two names, Turlough straightened to his full height and addressed Easten directly. "Your name, Easten is one I have not heard before, but it has a powerful ring! Perori is easier to place, especially if you are from Cymru, where the name simply means 'music'. You are from Cymru." Turlough didn't even try to make this sound like a question. Easten's respect and admiration for the dignity and bearing of the *seanch'ai* had risen in their brief interchange, now it took a gigantic step.

"My name is not common in Cymru, but my home is

close to the disputed lands that have as often been ruled from the Angles as they have been loyal to whichever lord of Cymru has been strong enough to take them in battle and call them his own. My name might easily have roots outside Cymru, but my heart and my loyalties are with my liege lord. I am here on his business, and his alone. But we will not speak of that here and now! Simon, is it possible for this wise man to join us at the table? Or perhaps I should say, do your customs permit me to make such a request?"

Simon nodded. "It has always been our custom that a guest's wishes be honoured if at all possible, and on occasions such as this our *seanch'ai* is always at my side. If your custom is similar, we may have more in common than I had suspected."

Before he had finished speaking an extra seat was placed at the top table and Turlough installed in his accustomed place with the pomp and ceremony befitting his important role in the community.

The feast was leisurely, interrupted by frequent pauses for toasts. For practical reasons, the covered tureens and plates offering warm food were tackled first, followed by the cold cuts and other delicacies served on a variety of breads, many unfamiliar to Easten. A stream of singers and other entertainers performed. As the last light of the day faded, torches were lit and placed all around; the smoke from these smelt sweet, not acrid.

The mountains of food gradually reduced, but there was no noticeable reduction in liquid refreshment, which circulated as freely as ever. There was a slight but noticeable pause in the entertainments, and Simon turned to Easten.

"I think now might be a good time for you to introduce your 'travel companion'—and I'm not referring to the ones wi' two legs!" he added, with a disarming grin.

As Easten stood, conversations around the town square came to a halt; he realised they had been waiting for this moment, but had allowed him to eat, drink and enjoy their unstinted, welcoming hospitality. He lifted Perori from her place of honour with due deference and cradled her lovingly.

"Dear friends, I cannot thank you enough for the welcome you have given my companions and myself! I'm sure many of you wonder how I can be making myself understood even though I have never been here before or learnt your language.

"As I have already told your Harbour Master, there is no sorcery involved, nor any of the Dark Arts. What has made it possible for me to speak to you is a unique gift, freely given first to me, and later to my Norse guides, then to your Harbour Master, Simon and his assistants and now most recently yourselves.

"However, the generous giver of this precious skill with languages is unable to speak to you herself or explain why she has chosen to assist us in understanding each other, as she has no tongue or voice and must perforce speak through a third party. I am honoured that I appear to have found favour in her eyes!

"Among my... people," Easten hesitated. He sensed the word he had chosen was not the best. But he had to continue... "Among my Tribe—clan might be a better term!—there is an ancient custom still followed, whereby a truly beautiful item may be honoured with a name, as if it were a living, breathing entity with an independent nature.

"Your *seanch'ai* Turlough recognised this at once, without needing any long explanations from me!" He laid his hand across Perori's strings and let his gaze travel slowly around the room. Perori throbbed, a deep and powerful major chord. "This truly remarkable 'wise man' knew without being told that her name is Perori, which in the language of the people who raised me means 'Music'.

"In some way I have yet to understand myself, it appears that through music, Perori may grant the gift of language skills to those who ask and are deemed worthy." Reading the expressions on the upturned faces, Easten knew he'd been successful, gaining the confidence of all present. His fingers stirred, though he had not consciously decided on a melody to demonstrate Perori's range and the quality of the music locked within her. The first notes floated from the dais placed carefully to give the honour guests dining there a few significant inches advantage of height over the assembled villagers and a panoramic view of the quayside that had been temporarily transformed into an al fresco feasting hall. The phrases and strands of music danced above the heads of the assembled diners, growing in volume, circling the treetops, and returning with renewed vigour to entrance and beguile the audience. An awed hush settled over the gathering. Nobody moved. Every person breathed as shallowly as possible, making a conscious effort to make no noise.

Easten was swept along with the wild, free swoops of the music as it climaxed in an impossible rush of notes that sparkled like pure diamonds, enhanced by the living flames of the torches, the only remaining light source in the full dark of a moonless night. His fingers slowed, his finely tuned senses and feelings for the 'rightness' of the melody told him when to play the final cadence to bring the piece to a perfect conclusion. When the last of the fading echoes of the music sighed, the silence that settled over the diners was absolute. Even the myriad natural sounds of the night—sleepy bird calls, the faintest rustles from the leaves on the trees—was stilled. Easten's heart was hammering. Perhaps five eternal seconds ticked past long enough for him to snatch two long, slow gasps of air, pumping fresh breath to his air-starved lungs before an anonymous member of the crowd broke the silence with a thunderclap of hands, showing his or her appreciation and thanks. Less than a second later everyone else reacted in similar fashion, adding foot stamps and a rhythmic beating of fists on the table surface to cries of appreciation and peals of laughter.

"That was a truly masterful show of your talent my friend!" said Simon.

"You do me too great an honour, Sire; the true talent is not mine, but belongs to Perori. In many ways, I am but her bearer and servant; I sometimes believe she plays me, rather than the reverse!"

"You take no credit for the composition of the music we have just... I hesitate to say merely 'heard', perhaps 'experienced' would be closer to the mark?"

"Sir, that composition was not one of my poor efforts—nor any other musician I have met or studied, living or dead! To my knowledge it has no name, no provenance. I believe it to be a newly composed piece and entirely of Perori's making, heard for the first time here, tonight. 'Twould not be the first instance she has both surprised and delighted me in such a fashion!"

Simon made no protest, merely nodding as he turned to speak a few quiet words with Turlough. He then raised his arms in a gesture that clearly called the meeting to a semblance of order. It was clear all were accustomed to instant obedience of commands issued by the Harbour Master.

When a silence was restored, he waved Turlough to stand and deliver the community's thanks and appreciation.

"I have heard many musicians through the years; local children who have grown to become the minstrels who play at feasts, weddings and wakes, and also wandering troubadours who have visited us and left us the legacy of new music from each of the Seven Kingdoms of Eire.

"Today we have heard from another musician, the first to visit these shores from the land in the east, shared by our cousins in Cymru and the varied tribes of Angles, Sacsen, Viking and others who have settled there— mostly, but not entirely (or so I have been told) in relative harmony!"

He paused, with a wicked gleam of childish humour in his eyes and let a ripple of amusement make its way around the tables. "Our honoured guest is far too modest about his own skills! He claims that the beauty of the music we have just heard comes from the instrument he carries, which he names Perori. But I say: the two cannot be divided, as even the most beautiful, perfectly crafted instrument needs a competent player to release such exquisite sounds! Easten, we salute you and thank you for your musical skills and welcome you to our fold. Would you consent to playing another piece for us to enjoy?"

Easten had anticipated the request. "I would ask one

thing of you, that my companion and guide on the journey, Palle, be allowed to play a duet. He is at least as skilled as I and known among his own people as a master of his craft. He deserves acknowledgement!"

Palle stood and bowed, his instrument at hand. Easten played a gentle riff of half a dozen notes as Palle struck a chord that gave depth to the phrase, and they were both lost in the intricate patterns of melody that sprang from their respective instruments. After moments, Palle segued into a Norse melody Easten could vaguely recall, and nodded for Palle to take the lead, content to accompany him. They reached a secondary melody he recognised as a recurring refrain; as they played, he was aware of voices being raised.

The singing voices were all firmly bass and baritone; Easten realised the singers had to be the Norse settlers and the injured seamen who had been left behind to recuperate. Once again, Perori's influence played a part and he was able to understand as they sang of their love of the sea and sailing, and the battles they had fought. Before the song ended, he could also hear trills and chirrups from flutes and other reedy instruments making their contributions, and the insistent underlying rhythm of a drum. The term *bhodran* was 'there' in his consciousness. Somehow, he knew this was the Irish name for the flat, circular hand-beaten drum.

The evening continued with song and drink, and platters of food reappeared from time to time. The music swiftly took the upper hand and several cheerful groups had set themselves up in open competition, with good-natured ragging and chaffing intended to keep each group on their toes and offer their best efforts for the ongoing entertainment.

The music mellowed with the evening, becoming more relaxed, softening in style, slowing to reflect the mood and ambience. There came a point when, for the first time, there was a natural pause in the songs, ballads, poetry, juggling and other entertainments which had continued nonstop throughout the meal. With a glance at Simon, Turlough rose and struck the wooden dais three times with his staff. All conversation stilled.

Easten shot a puzzled look at Simon, who leaned across and murmured, "The midnight hour approaches. We have a tradition of ending our feasts with a certain song, led by our *seanch'ai*."

Turlough turned to face the North Star, which sparkled brighter than every other diamond in the sky and appeared to rest exactly on the tip of the tallest of the surrounding trees. Raising both arms he began a verse, praising the beauty of Nature, the bounty of the fields and forests and the seasons of the year. The song was over all too soon for Easten, who had hoped for several verses. As the final notes drifted lazily upwards, borne on the smoke of the last embers of the cooking fires, the people at the general boards placed arms around the shoulders of their closest neighbour. The men sat at the Head Table crossed arms and grasped the hand of the person next to them. Easten's sensitive ears caught an occasional murmur from one or two of them, but the majority made their adieus in silence before retiring to his own lodging.

CHAPTER EIGHT

"The hour may be late, but there are matters we must discuss if you wish to make an early start on your Quest tomorrow."

The last of the guests ambled home, leaving the almost-bare tables to be cleared and cleansed later in the day.

Easten had hoped for this opportunity but considering the lateness of the hour he had not expected the elderly *seanch'ai* to suggest continuing to discuss practical matters at the end of a day that had been so long and arduous.

Where does the old man find the energy? he wondered, but was too polite to speak his thoughts.

Turlough turned to him and smiled.

"Your inner thoughts cannot hurt or offend me," he said, with a short, almost silent lilt of laughter in his voice. He caught the surprise in Easten's eyes and turned away Easten's attempts to protest his innocence. "In the many years since I was honoured to become the *seanch'ai*, I have heard far worse thoughts—both overtly spoken, and those which the person in whose conscious thoughts they arose believed they had managed to conceal deep under the surface of their minds. To hide anything of your thoughts will cost you considerable effort, I promise, and you won't hide anything from me for long! I have had years of practice dealing with such matters, years you cannot hope to match! Be honest, my friend, and it will be to your advantage; I assure you, there is nothing to be gained from deceit!"

"By the cross I bear, I would not seek to lie to you!" Easten vowed, with sincerity. "I am already indebted to you and your people for the hospitality you have given us this night, and my journey is far from over. I am charged to deliver a message from my liege lord to his brother, as swiftly as possible. My companion, Palle, will travel with me when I leave. He has skill with languages, and we thought this would be a boon. At the time we had no idea how valuable Perori would prove!

"My lord is pressed on all sides by another who has powerful forces, and threatens to overrun my lord's lands…" In as few words as possible Easten explained the purpose of his appointed task. "…and so I must continue my journey at first light. I will be grateful if you can spare Palle and myself some assistance; perhaps a pack animal and supplies? If all goes as smoothly as I hope and pray, we will return along the same route before the moon has run a full cycle. I hope to have a healthy show of arms marching with me, but they will not be your enemies. Rather, the assistance my liege lord has begged his brother to send in support. Palle's chieftain, Erik, has provided two longships he deems enough to transport a fair-sized fighting force, but I promise you they will not harm a single hair on the head of your… followers? Tribe? Clan? I must confess I know not your customs and I have no wish to offend with an incautious remark!"

Turlough smiled. "The Clan do not 'follow' an old man who was never battle trained, even when I was still young! Yes, they will listen to me, whether I speak sanity or madness, but they will always 'follow'—in the sense I think you mean!—their own battle chief, Cormac! He is away on a hunting trip, and the flames tell me he is at least two days' hard riding from home. He's aware of your arrival but cannot reach Dubh Lyn before you say you must leave. Perhaps it is written you will meet when you return, perhaps not. I cannot scan that far into a future not yet written that may still be altered by events we can neither avoid nor imagine."

"You have some foreknowledge of events, then."

"Some have suggested as much to me, but many times the signs are all there for he who knows how to read them!"

"So your Warrior Chief is hunting, yet from the feast you provided at such short notice, you do not appear to want for supplies to last you through the winter months?"

"Cormac rides with the *Fianna*, securing the borders of our realm against any who might be tempted to annexe a defenceless outlying village…"

Easten held up one hand, as might a child uncertain of an instruction from his master. "Your pardon, but there is a word Perori cannot translate …"

"The Fianna? No, that is an ancient term, even for a language such as ours! I'm not surprised you and she cannot agree on a word (or even a whole phrase!) in substitute.

"They are a secretive folk who inhabit a world that physically is neither ours, nor completely separated. They are akin to the race you refer to in children's stories as the Fairies but they are real not imaginary, and there are certainly as many evil characters as good! On certain days of every year (which you call Midsummer and All

Hallows Eve) the veil between the two worlds is thin, very thin, and at such times there are many more who see apparitions pass from one side to the other, perhaps for a few hours or until the next time the veil is stretched to its thinnest and they are able to return."

"But the Faerie world…" Easten protested.

Turlough shook his head firmly. "Whatever you may have heard, you must forget! The Fianna are real and exert a great influence on our daily lives. Most are well-disposed to those of this world who have chosen to honour them as we do, but there are some who play cruel tricks on their victims, either for their own amusement or simply because they can!

"Cormac has built a good relationship with their leader, Fionn, and they often ride the borders of Tara and Moylurg to keep our boundaries secure."

"Is there anything Palle and I might do to beg their indulgence, persuade them to allow us a safe passage?"

Turlough's eyes softened in the fading light from the candles still burning on the Top Table. "A shrewd question, my friend, and from your tone I cannot doubt your sincerity! I would suggest you might use your natural talents for music. The Fianna sometimes appear to be a mass of contradictions. They are renowned for their fighting skills but also for their love of practical jokes and these can sometimes appear childish, inappropriate for a race of folk who generally live such long lives, by mortal standards. The one thing that defines them, however, is their love of music. I believe you will find your natural talents extremely useful on your journey.

"However, the hour is late! I advise you to take rest for what remains of the night. The journey ahead will be a long one on foot, but I'm sure we can make the road easier for you by providing two horses, and some of our travel food. I'm sure you'd prefer to keep moving, rather than stop at the wayside to cook meals!"

Turlough had started to cross the now-deserted open area as he spoke. Easten and Palle had automatically fallen into step, and discovered they had stopped outside a bothy no different to any of the others in the vicinity, but Turlough was sure this building was the one. He pulled aside a curtain to keep out draughts and indicated they enter. The furnishings were minimal, but cared for: two beds, topped with neatly folded linen and blankets, and a carefully banked, well-tended fire set long enough to heat the single room.

"May you sleep well this night, and every night on your Quest! I may not be up to offer my blessings when you leave; alas, these old bones insist on being treated with more respect than I was prepared to fritter on creature comforts when I was younger! I sense your journey has a noble purpose, and will be rewarded with… whatever you seek. Fear not! None have breathed a word out of turn! I merely voice my thoughts, based on what I have observed of the unlikely pairing of two skilful musicians travelling far from home clearly charged with bearing something to someone. It was not difficult to guess the person you would meet by travelling West from Dubh Lyn is none other than the High King at Tara, Dermot. You identified him straightway when you announced his kinship with a Princeling in Cymru, without mentioning the name of either man!"

"I see we must learn to guard our tongues, maybe even conceal our actions, hide our emotions, disguise our voices, alter our clothing…"

"No, my friend: you must be as natural as possible if you wish to avoid drawing judgement and suspicion on our heads. The more you try to 'act the part' you think others expect to see the more obvious the attempt at deceit, and you are more than likely to betray yourselves before a single day passes!"

Turlough sketched a formal benediction over the two musicians. Both were glad of it, tracing the Christian sign on their bodies as Turlough draped the curtain back in place and left them to settle as best they might.

"I had not realised the Christian faith had reached into the Norse communities," Easten remarked as they rolled into their blankets.

"We have had our share of travelling brothers visit the banks of the Maersee, even in the short time since we established a camp there," Palle replied. "And for myself, I'll accept any chance of blessing or good fortune on our mission, wherever it may come from! The cross I sign on my head, shoulders and heart is not so different from the Viking tradition of warding the vulnerable points of the body and anointing them with oil or grease before engaging in battle!"

Heavy breathing slowing into a deep, regular rhythm wafted from Easten's palliasse before Palle had completed his reply. He smiled and turned his face from the steady flicker of flame. He soon followed Easten into a dreamless sleep.

CHAPTER NINE

Easten was roused gently by the appealing fragrance from a hot infusion of herbs in a cup placed on a small table at the side of his bed. Cup was perhaps a misnomer, it was wide enough at the brim to be called a bowl and had to contain at least a pint of… whatever it was. Easten sniffed it and looked up at Simon with a question in his eyes.

Simon smiled. "Tay, is what we call it; herbs steeped in hot water. Tasty, and 'twill chase any mists of the night that remain. Take your time, enjoy it: we may break our fast with a hearty warm meal to send you on your way, but our kitchen's overlord informs me it will be a few minutes before the meal is ready!"

Palle rolled over and eased up on one elbow. "Smells good. I think I recognise some of the herbs, but not by name." Easten took a cautious sip; it had cooled enough for him to hold the liquid in his mouth a moment before swallowing. "Tastes as good as it smells!" He had to restrain himself from the temptation to empty the contents of the goblet in a single draught.

Palle raised his oversized chalice in a mock-formal toast: Easten caught his mood and copied the gesture. They drank together and took the empty vessels with them as they went in search of solid sustenance.

Bowls of porage sweetened with berries were waiting, but it was far superior to the travel fare the unknown cook on Erik's longship could produce: hardly surprising, considering the conditions the sea cook had had to contend with. Thick slices of meat left over from the feast evening were served cold, alongside four different styles of bread from the oven and hot enough to partly melt pats of fresh-churned butter that were a little too close on the crowded table. An enormous slab of cheese completed the bill of fare, apart from two tall porcelain containers covered with fresh, clean muslin cloths, which on investigation proved to contain more of the unfamiliar but tasty hot beverage.

"I don't think I'll eat again this next sevenday!" Easten declared, wiping his fingers on a hot towel an attentive young boy had placed in his hands as he pushed back his chair and bowed his thanks to Simon at the head of the table.

"I agree," Palle added as he strove to follow Easten's lead.

Simon acknowledged the courteous gesture from both guests with a polite demurral.

"I cannot say how safe you will find the road as you travel West, but the first two or three days should be well ordered; you should make good progress." He clapped, and two sleek, frisky horses were led into the clearing by young boys of nine or ten. "These horses are fleet of foot, yet known to be a safe ride; you do ride, I take it?"

Both nodded, gazing approvingly at the horseflesh. Easten didn't trust himself to speak for fear of blurting tears, of gratitude or some less masculine emotion. He had the distinct impression that the generous gesture Simon's people made had affected his travel companion in a similar fashion.

"You will find the panniers have been filled with a number of foods that travel well without spoiling and can be eaten as you find them. Some can also be reheated, should you decide to break your journey long enough to build a fire and cook, but I'm sure you won't need telling which are more nutritious eaten hot. There is a small amount of cereal—oats, as it happens—that may be useful if you are forced to stop somewhere with poor or nonexistent forage for the horses, though I doubt you will be forced to overnight in mountainous regions where the grass is sparse. If you pass unhindered, and find good grazing, you can eat the oats yourselves in a porage. Finally, fill up your water flasks at the first stream; there will be plenty along the way but remember to keep them filled—especially during the last hour of each day, so you have water through the night!"

With Simon's well-intentioned 'advice' in their ears, Easten and Palle rode out of the village just after daybreak. As Simon had promised, the road was hard-packed and easy to follow, as it branched neither to the left nor right but directly West, where the backdrop was provided by a mountain range.

"Once we are close at hand, you will discover we can slip between ranges of these mountains rather than force a long, cold march to the top and back down."

"Surely this is one place any enemy—of the physical variety, or from the world of the Fey—can be expected to challenge us, test our strength and resolution, pin us in a trap and fall on us with superior numbers?"

"If they do, we must be ready to defend ourselves! The relics we carry are small enough to be concealed if we wish…"

"Turlough told us the first part of our journey was on a safe route, Palle. We must trust that he was right."

"He also told us of the Færy folk and seemed convinced they are just as real as you and me! Do you believe an elderly man's word, one who believes in the folk legends he cites as if part of the country's history?"

"This much I will say, my friend. Turlough has lived a long and varied life, and not achieved that by living in the realms of fantasy and tales told to children at bedtime! I have seen and heard things I cannot explain away, and I am therefore more than willing to keep an open mind about the existence of the Fianna. We are strangers in this land, we should not be too hasty to discount the possibility Færy folk do indeed inhabit it. Remember, Turlough also told us they are a force for Good, even those not inclined to help have a reputation for mischief or trickery rather than showing a disposition for Evil."

The weather was kind: warm and dry. They had a well-trodden road. Their horses were fresh and they made good time. The road bent slowly from the range of mountains on their left, leading them a few points north of west.

Towards noon they paused before crossing a small river where a ford had been created by a careful laying of regularly sized smooth stones, visible just below the surface and free of slippery moss or other plant life. Words were unnecessary: it was the best place to rest and eat under the shade of the trees, protected from the midday sun.

"This is the sort of place I could easily imagine the Færy folk of Turlough's tales might be found," Palle said as he investigated the contents of one of the panniers strapped across his mount's withers.

"I see several rings of mushrooms. In stories I have heard they are often claimed to be associated with certain Fey—usually as hiding places, or even homes! I wonder if these are safe to eat?"

"Have a care, Easten! As you have said, we are not familiar with the plants and animals native to this country. I have heard stories of people who have become ill from eating the wrong sort of mushroom: some can cause death!"

Easten returned from the stream with two dripping waterskins and passed one to Palle. "It seems Turlough was right about this first part of the road."

Palle's eyes widened; he made an unobtrusive hand signal for Easten to continue walking towards him. His gaze was focussed on something (or someone) beyond Easten, who felt an urge to spin around. Something in Palle's tense body language told him that this was not the best thing to do, right now. An itch was developing, demanding to be scratched, between his shoulder blades, reminding him of his vulnerability. He had to make a conscious effort to take the final steps towards a tree where he slumped to the ground and used the rough bole to ease his discomfort. He scanned the open ground across the stream they would soon cross but saw nothing untoward.

Opening his satchel, he put his head down to rummage inside and whispered, "You saw something?"

"A movement. Still, perhaps it was no more than the tail of a jumping fish. It was just downstream from the crossing..." Palle murmured. He was also hiding his lip movements behind the flap of his provisions sack.

"There it is again! No jumping fish, I'm certain this

time!"

With the clue of where to concentrate his gaze, Easten saw it too.

"I swear I saw a pair of eyes, between that clump of rushes, but no human could lie concealed in so few inches of water!"

"If we are being observed, it's the first sign of anyone showing us any interest. In fact, I can't remember seeing anyone close enough to hail since we left Dubh Lyn. Your thoughts?"

"No sudden movements. There may be more eyes upon us, and we don't want to appear a threat."

"Agreed! But we should not appear hostile intruders on someone's private land, either. This ford is obviously tended and may mark a boundary. Let us try something."

Without waiting for a reply, Palle stood and raised his food pouch in one hand; the other he held open, palm forwards, showing (he hoped) he carried no weapon. "We mean no trespass and no harm, my friend! Will you not show yourself, come forward and share our midday meal?"

For several tense seconds there was no response. "We have also something more flavoursome than spring water to drink!" Easten added, pulling a leathern bottle from his pack. "Please join us, we are but travellers and would welcome company—perhaps a guide?—on a road neither of us know well."

The eyes reappeared briefly. Easten was pleased to know that he had been peering intently at almost the exact point on the far bank of the stream where the eyes had been concealed. A figure rose from the rushes, perhaps three feet from the crown of golden tresses that surrounded an old-young face with the most disturbingly ice-blue eyes he had seen. A female face, he decided, though there was little to confirm or deny this in the clothing the creature wore, which resembled more fish scales than any tailored garb. The apparition had arms, short but in perfect proportion to her (its?) height, and the nether region had a greenish tinge rather than the tanned torso. It carried no obvious weapon and stood on feet rather than balancing on a tail.

"*Dia duit! Croeso*—and welcome!" Easten called, using the commonest greetings he could recall from the languages he had used most on his journey. The creature stepped onto the near shore and spread both arms as she bowed and demonstrated her lack of weapons. As she bowed—almost a formal curtsey, Easten thought—two more figures appeared from the bushes upstream of the crossing, and two more downstream. Once again (and still without understanding why) Easten sensed that, although unquestionably of the same (type? race? family?) these four were without question male.

"You are all welcome to share our meal. We have plenty to offer! Join us, please!"

He had no idea yet of how far they had left to travel (or even if they would be allowed to continue) but not to share travel food would be churlish ill manners in any society Easten had lived among or briefly visited, and he had no qualms about it. After all, he told himself, it cannot be too far; from what details he remembered of the available maps, Ros Comyn was barely three days from Dubh Lyn on foot, and they had the advantage of horses.

Easten and Palle found themselves consciously willing one of the five to indicate some comprehension and was relieved when one of the upstream 'males' grinned and offered him an open hand. Before Easten could react, the more feminine central figure cast a sharp glance at the companion on her right. He lowered his hand and looked embarrassed.

The sprite stepped forwards, clearly considering herself spokesperson and leader for the group. Stepped was perhaps too prosaic a word to describe the fluidity of her motion. Her feet appeared to dance across the surface of the water, weightless, not leaving the least suggestion of touching the eternally mobile currents and eddies. As she reached the near shore, there was no hint of dampness on the powder dry smooth pebbles she walked on. In defiance of logic, she appeared to have crossed the stream dry-shod.

"You are also thrice welcome, stranger, but why the repeated greeting? Is this a custom of your Clan?"

"Indeed, I assure you it is not! The people of my native Cymru have developed a reputation as a folk of few words, never using two if one will suffice! But I was not aware I might have been 'over-egging' my greetings. All I did was use the words of welcome in the three most widely understood languages we have encountered on our journey in the hope you might perhaps understand enough of just one of them and realise we come not as enemies, but as friends."

"I hear that you are not native to these parts, but I cannot place your accents! You speak the Gael, but in a manner I have not heard… are you perhaps from the south, from Cobh or Kerry? Or are you recently returned from a longer voyage, across the grey seas?"

Easten smiled and shook his head. "My companion, Palle, is from the frozen lands of the north, and has travelled many more miles than I, for this is my first trip from the town where I grew up. He has briefly visited this beautiful country once before. How long ago would that have been, Palle?"

"That was about the time my son was born; he has now seen two summers and two winters pass. But I was here for less than a summer moon and had little opportunity to learn more than a few chance words of the spoken language."

A frown of suspicion appeared on the brow of the spokesperson. "How, then, is it possible for me to understand every word you speak so clearly? And I sense I should be including my brothers, as they also closely follow all you say!"

Four silent nods confirmed this.

"Yet when I watch your lip movements, they do not correspond with the sounds I hear. What trickery is this? Is there sorcery involved, or one of the Dark Arts?"

"Peace, friend!" Easten protested. "I cannot explain the "how" of your question, but I will gladly relate for you what I have learnt… though I fear it will prove not worth a great deal. As I have already said I come from Cymru, across the sea, a land where music is held to be precious. You are not the first to discover you can understand a language you have never before heard spoken or read or had opportunity to study! I cannot explain how, but can only aver it has happened several times already on our journey, short though it may have been!"

By now Easten had become skilled at summarising the benefits of Perori's gift of languages, and somehow managing to persuade any listener more terrified of the concept of sorcery than the advantages of learning a new skill that it was not for the sake of a tidbit of dangerous knowledge, but that Perori offered a genuine only of benefit to all who applied it wisely.

"And although we understand little of what is happening, we're convinced Perori is not a sorcerer's tool, but a force for peace and harmony."

The figure faced her companions, whom she had now identified as her brothers. A brief silence followed during which they were clearly communing with each other in a manner transcending the need for more mundane matters such as an audible conversation. At last the lead figure turned to include them once more in the decision.

"My brothers and I can sense the "rightness" of your words and could never doubt them. We have no difficulty accepting your curious tale, unlikely though it may seem, as we have seen in our long and eventful lives many things which cannot be explained away in simple, everyday terms."

"Yet we have been somewhat lacking in extending you the courtesy you gave us, the knowledge of your names…"

"No, you should not think that!"

Palle was fractionally the swifter to react; Easten nodded for him to continue.

"We are, after all, the strangers in this beautiful country of yours. You have nothing more than our unsupported word that we are not spies for a potential enemy thinking to attack. Also, we cannot ask for testimony from another, someone you might know and trust.

"We would be honoured if you would share a simple meal with us: it may be that the breaking of bread will help us establish a relationship. We can learn something of each others' ways, and it will allow us to relate for you the reasons for our journey, and you will have plenty of time to tell us as much or little of yourselves as you decide prudent to reveal to two unknown travellers."

Once they had eaten their fill, they had all relaxed sufficiently to accept each other as friends. As Easten had instinctively guessed, the female sprite was the 'senior member': the term "Leader" was one which they recognised, but either would or could not apply to themselves or the ways of their… family, clan, race: even a direct mental query aimed at Perori, disrobed and gleaming in the afternoon sunshine during the exchange of courtesies, was inconclusive. The five beings were siblings, as their spokesperson stated before they sat to eat: they were all from the one set of parents.

"I was aware, Easten, that you had understood how my brothers and I stood and spoke to each other's minds for a few moments when you told us something of how we were able to understand each other. For us it's a simple, practical way of doing things: we don't have to be physically close, we speak in confidence to each other, or to the whole set at once if we prefer. We have no secrets; as family, why should we?"

"Yet for this reason, we have never felt the need for individual names; we always know who we speak to, and only need to interact with others on rare occasions. You are the first Mortals we have met who have invited us to share a meal, and as you are accustomed to using individual, personal names it seems only fair to arrange to help you. You may call me Sí, which in our tongue would be a 'name' to fit any female of our type…" (There, again, was that curious 'feel' of a word that lacked an accurate translation.)

"For my brothers, the simplest would be to name them in the order of their birth: One, Two, Three, Four. They are content with this, and if it makes things easier for you for as long as we share the road…"

"Are you offering to travel part of our way with us?" exclaimed Easten. Something deep in his conscious mind insisted this was an offer he had dared to imagine, not daring to think it might be so freely offered without having to ask.

"We feel the 'rightness' of your words, and the reason for your journey. Why would we wish to make things difficult for someone of pure heart who seeks to perform noble deeds for anther unable to help himself? We are from a different origin; we are 'in' this mortal world but have never been 'of' it, despite the time we have lived here amongst other races and people, and we are very long-lived!"

"For all these reasons—and possibly for none!—we as the Fey people mortals sometimes perceive us to be can choose to follow one path or another and often do exactly that. We follow our fancy; most Mortal folk are unaware of our existence, and the few we encounter more sensitive to our presence have not the imagination—or possibly the courage!—to take the final step, accept that they can never hope to 'own' a whole world as they fondly imagine they do!

"You speak of the 'honour' of sharing a meal with us: we have decided it would be just as real an honour to be permitted to escort you through this realm, act as your guides, safeguard you against surprise or danger. The noble nature of your purpose in riding to assist another deserves

acknowledgement and reward!"

Easten felt it was up to him to accept this unlooked-for assistance. As musician and lyricist, an acceptance speech, however short, deserved some formal structuring but he was genuinely unsure how to phrase it. Sí looked him directly in the eye as these thoughts and several others tumbled haphazardly across his mind. She smiled, without a trace of mockery.

"The sincerity you have already shown, which I read in your mind as easily as if you were to shout it from the highest peak, is without price! We believe you deserve all the assistance you need."

Put in such simple, sincere terms, Easten discovered (to his surprise) it was easier to accept this offer, so freely given by Sí and on behalf of her less voluble siblings, than he could have imagined.

Automatically he raised his eyes to the heavens. His intention had been to murmur a sincere thanks, He was distracted by what he saw: despite the leisurely nature of their meal, the sun still stood at its zenith, high above. A frown knitted his brow.

Sí glanced up, responding as if he had put the query in his mind into words. "You guessed at once—and correctly! —that my brothers and I are 'in' this world, without being fully 'of' it. That has advantages from time to time, and being in our company has made it possible for you to share in some, it would seem!

"Time is of less importance or significance for us than for the Mortal races of this world. You have made it clear your business on this journey is of vital importance to another—many others—who depend on the wellbeing of the lord you serve so selflessly and well! Time, you have admitted, is of the essence for the success of your quest: it's as good a reason as any to be grateful for the slowing of time's passage, for as long as we are your invited guests at a meal!"

Compared with some of the new things he had learnt and experienced in the past few days, the idea that something as fixed and predictable as the dance of the hours and days that built into a framework of regularly recurring months and predictable years becoming 'movable feasts' wasn't as difficult to accept; Easten absorbed the premise of a more elastic malleability to the concept of Time.

Hard on the heels of this came another thought, one he was still trying to pin in the form of a second query: again, Sí was there before he could speak.

"It would take you years of practice before you could hope to conceal your thoughts from me, my siblings, or any of our race, the Fianna! But you have my word, we would never dream of intruding on your privacy, or enter your mind and listen to your inner thoughts uninvited! Now it is my turn to ask you to take this on trust, in similar fashion to your earlier request for us to accept your 'curious tale'. My brothers and I believe you have every right to all the privacy you need. Is this to your satisfaction?"

"Indeed, it is more than we could ever have expected!"

Easten was buoyed by confidence that the chances of his mission succeeding had improved another significant notch. With a glance to Palle, he began repacking the items of uneaten travel food : Palle repacked his provender sacks. They had not stinted during their midday meal, but for some reason there was a significant amount of food remaining on the blanket they had spread as an impromptu feast table even when the packs and sacks were full to capacity.

"Call it our… contribution to an excellent meal!" came an immediate riposte in Sí's now familiar 'voice' inside Easten's head, accompanied by a lengthy peal of merry laughter. The extra food items blinked out of sight, and small sacks of the sort carried by travellers everywhere appeared on the shoulders of all four sprite brothers, who laughed as if someone had just told them the funniest of jokes.

"And yet why not?" Easten thought, calmly. After all, if being in proximity to his beloved Perori was sufficient to make communication possible between people who spoke different languages, or create Peace where once hostility and mistrust held sway, and even test how far the elasticity of something so fixed as Time might be stretched, it was surely not unreasonable to discover that the remains left after a substantial meal could expand to become more than what had been shared. One of the stories told during his instruction before accepting the new religion came to mind. Something of this nature must have happened when the Messiah figure preached to over five thousand people. He remembered reading that many baskets had been filled with leftover food, though only five small loaves and a couple of fish had been blessed…

"It pleases me that you can accept this, friend Easten! The story you have been told is one I have also heard, but as far as I know none of the Fianna were involved on that occasion. If they had been, the story would have had a place in the records and tales passed from one generation of our race to the next, and I would have heard it from someone when I was young and still in training.

"Also: when we travel, we travel swiftly and light. We need no more than the light of the moon at night, the wind in our hair and the sun on our faces. Pure water from a convenient stream as we pass completes our needs from day to day, and this must be borne in mind when considering the worth of the meal you offered us so freely."

Sí opted to make her thoughts audible—though her lip movements confirmed that the language she was using—presumably 'the Gael' as she had already, repeatedly called it—was not the words he was 'hearing' through the delicate bones and membrane designed to make the general hearing process possible. She paused to make sure she had Easten's and Palle's attention before she carried on. She spoke with unquestionable sincerity, "The *seanch'ai* who counselled you in Dubh Lyn, Turlough, is a wise and ancient man. We have known of him for many years, and although he is more sensitive and receptive than most, I do not think he has yet sensed our presence, though we have kept a watchful eye on him through the years."

"He was right when he told you that the first stage of your journey would be free from dangers of any sort. The paths you have trodden he knows well, and he has trodden them himself enough times.

"Once we cross this stream, we will be leaving the realm of the King in Dubh Lyn and entering the realm of Tara, which owes its allegiance to your lord's brother, the High King Cormac Rú. For the moment, there is peace between the Seven Kingdoms in Erin, and of the seven Tara is the largest and most powerful.

"We can flex the passage of time to ensure your remaining journey is trouble-free: at need, we can even conceal ourselves and any who travel with us—or suddenly reveal ourselves, if it appears that it would be to our advantage!

"My brothers and I know where you are headed. You have not tried to deceive me in that, and it would have been impossible for me not to know your mind, though I promise, I have not deliberately 'stolen' the knowledge against your wishes! It was too close to the surface of your mind and could not be concealed.

"Travelling close to us will not stop the passage of time—nothing can achieve that! But while we are together, we can manipulate the speed at which it flows, like dams in a river. In this way, we can help you complete your journey faster than possible if you were to attempt unaided. Is this acceptable?"

Easten nodded, knowing instinctively he could answer for Palle, too. He felt himself tremble on the verge of tears as gratitude nearly overwhelmed him.

"Then, let us away!" Sí cried. "We run, or swim, even sometimes fly, but we cannot be outpaced by any horse in this Mortal world! Should we come to a river that runs the way we travel, we may refresh ourselves in its cooling waters, but never more than one of us at a time: fear not that we might lose interest and leave you without warning, or unprotected. And remember, though we will remain visible, others will not sense our presence—and as promised, we will also cloak you from the sight of any we sense are hostile to you or your cause."

"We can only offer our deepest and most heartfelt thanks for your protection!" Easten managed to stammer.

His emotions were still playing havoc with his calm. He vaulted into his saddle. Before setting heel to his mount's flank he paused and added a final comment, "I will not ask it of you to accompany us all the way to King Cormac's court."

"I have made no attempt to hide my thoughts from you, so you must know Turlough himself warned me, Cormac can be a difficult person. He can be a friend in need, but also a suspicious and vengeful tyrant, and he has a network of informers throughout Tara who report to him on the gossip and trivial events they learn. Getting even close to the seat of his power on Lough Cé may not be as easy: it might even mean someone becoming aware of your existence, which I understand you would prefer not to happen!"

"There will be time for that decision when we are close to your goal, my friend," replied Sí. "At very least, we will make sure you are within sight of the castle before we discuss any further amendment of our plans!"

"Now, as far as time is concerned, we have held those sluice gates closed for as long as we dare; now is not a moment too soon for us to leave!"

Sí half-turned and stared hard back along the path Easten and Palle had followed from Dubh Lyn. A disorganised rabble appeared from the eaves of the forest, streaming down hill and picking up their tracks with apparent ease.

"I think they're probably still too far off to be able to see us!" Palle breathed, turning his mount, poised to flee on Easten's word.

"Agreed, but we should depart with speed!" Easten cried, prepared to lead off but waiting for Sí or one of her siblings to suggest the best direction for flight. They were clearly outnumbered, and this was never the fleeing of a coward, merely a prudent withdrawal, a necessary fact of any military person's professional life.

His boots had been designed for comfortable walking—all day if necessary. They had not been designed as riding apparel, and as a result he had neither goad nor spur to assist in controlling the horse. He decided he had to take the initiative and gave his steed's flanks a firm clip, hoping this would be sufficient to convince the horse who was really in charge, and what was required.

His mount obliged instantly, and in the manner Easten hoped.

He'd ridden a horse probably just as often as anyone from 'home'—wherever that was, he thought for a split-second before dismissing all thinking not directly and exclusively pertaining to riding skills and keeping out of sight from anyone so keen to track them down. They appeared to be carrying shields with a device Easten was convinced he ought to recognise, if only they were closer. How could that be, though? After all, this was the first time he had visited the country, Erin or Eire, depending on who you were talking to and where and when the conversation happened.

Slowly, gingerly at first, then with increasing confidence, his mount stepped daintily from one large, smooth pebble in the ford to the next. The stones were so carefully laid, so flat and smooth, they could not fail to prove that this site had been built by someone regularly cleaned and serviced to ensure it remained a secure and easily negotiated crossing point.

Under Easten's insistent hand, the horse picked

gingerly across. He'd hoped for the best, but prayed to be spared the worst. It seemed his wish would be granted. He reached the opposite bank—a maximum of perhaps twenty or twenty-five feet—and studied the two brothers who had opted to follow.

The graceful 'slide' (as opposed to "stride") was achieved by extending a questing bare foot as close as possible (and certainly no more than about two-three inches) over the running waters. A (water-soluble) paste had been spread on the soles of the feet of the person attempting the crossing, visual inspection would reveal that the soles of both feet remained dry.

Sí paused before following. Raising both arms she executed a sequence of graceful expressive movements while she danced lightly across the glade where they had rested and eaten. A light eddy of leaves swirled in her wake, mingling with a smaller number of fresh leaves which detached from the branches overhead, though it was far from autumn. Easten studied where he knew they had set a fire to heat their meal. Fresh, naturally green and luxuriant grass already covered the remaining cold cinders and soot-blackened grass.

Sí joined with them on the western bank, where they had sped to the temporary concealment afforded by the verges of a forest.

"It will not fool a trained tracker long, but it may buy us time. Nature has agreed to assist in concealing our tracks, and evidence of our recent presence."

They turned once more westwards and set off. This forest was different; most obviously in that there were no clear paths or tracks. Easten thought it likely that the forest itself was not a portion of a larger estate belonging to a single family or person, but developed in its own time as a natural habitat for wildlife.

"In that much you are right."

Easten wasn't prepared to hear his unspoken thoughts confirmed by Sí's low purr of approval inside his head: he stiffened in his saddle and had to make a conscious effort to relax. "No offence taken, milady, and none intended from me, but you startled me replying to a question I barely formed in my mind!"

"Indeed, there are things we both must learn of the other's habits to continue working together! I can reassure you, none could take offence from an apology so courteously worded! But now it is time we hasten. Stay close!"

Without waiting for a reply, Sí flowed in front of Easten's mount and leapt at a gap between two tree boles Easten was certain had not been apparent moments before. Instinctively he drummed his heels into the horse's flanks. The horse obeyed without question, and even more amazing they both passed between the two trees without snagging on any low branches. A path appeared to be opening silently and with perfect timing. Concentrating on keeping Sí in sight, together with judging what assistance his horse might require negotiating obstacles, he dared not glance back over his shoulder but suspected the path was just as silently closing again, concealing their direction.

As they sped along the non-existent track through a pathless virgin forest, Easten felt an odd sensation building. A small vein in his forehead throbbed gently and slowly as if he were trotting in a relaxed manner, enjoying light exercise in a favourite formal park. His breathing was slow and even: his horse, the same. They followed without hindrance every move made by the water sprite who led the party without risk of falling behind, or becoming lost in this maze of trees, and had plenty of time to keep her in constant view.

The evidence of his eyes told a different tale. While his pulse and muscles insisted he and his mount were moving at a sedate, leisurely pace, his eyes told him the trees and bushes on either side were disappearing behind them at a mind-stopping speed, far too fast for safety even on a well-made public road, suicidal when attempted through a trackless forest unknown and untested by any of the party. He hunched closer to the horse's neck and tried to peer forwards, beyond Sí's lithe form as she slid as gracefully as ever between trees which again in a split-second eased aside in perfect time. The horse showed no weariness and from time to time one or other of the sibling brothers would appear briefly at his side, waving encouragement and smiling before dropping back to his accustomed place. None were in physical discomfort.

At last they came to the forest's eaves. The first clue Easten had was the faintest of cooling breezes caressing his cheek, carrying with it the scent of meadow flowers that overlaid the tang of the still forest air they had been breathing for… how many hours? Easten looked up and noted that according to the sun it was still mid-afternoon. That couldn't be right; is it even the same day?

"The answer to both questions is "Yes", my friend! There are many seemingly impossible things in this Mortal world of yours that cannot be explained away: it has been claimed a wise man will try his best to believe ten of them before breakfast!"

Sí's comment was encased in a package of almost out-of-control chuckles and laughter that would have without question persuaded the most dismal, depressed, and lonely person to smile. For Easten it was akin to receiving a shot of adrenaline combined with the tingle of pleasure and anticipation felt when plunging into the depths of a cold pool in the middle of a hot summer day.

Roughly to the north, on their right as they galloped at breakneck speed beyond the last few trees, a river meandered unhurriedly past, bending around to flow in their direction, a few points north of west.

Sí trotted to Easten's side as one brother whooped for joy and hared off to plunge into the river. Easten noted that however long they'd been running and riding though the forest, she showed no signs of distress; she wasn't even breathing heavily.

"We have made excellent time through Moylurg," she said, "and I think it will be difficult—if not impossible!—for anyone to follow the chase we led through those woods. But we cannot relax yet: our journey is not at an end, and we must maintain speed. We are deep within Tara, a region my brothers and I rarely visit, and our powers are less strong this far from our home.

"Continue to make the speed you can and remain within sight of the river. We will all take the opportunity to refresh mind and body in our preferred medium, the living waters of the river! There will always be three or four of us to keep you company and ward you from surprise!"

Without waiting for a reply (which Easten decided wasn't strictly necessary) she left his side and resumed her deceptively fast, powerful, ground-eating lope across the free open meadowland. A short distance downstream the river bent slightly north, and the first of the siblings opted to emerge here. With a loud whoop of cheer (and more than likely, Easten thought, an equally loud mental shout he couldn't hear) she made fluttering gestures to her brother as she hared off like an excited child to claim her reward, flinging herself into the river. Easten had to assume Sí had made the first bather temporary leader, as he settled into her position at the head of the line and set a cracking pace. Despite now being on open ground, Easten found he had to concentrate to keep the deputised sibling in sight.

Over open ground it was not easy to make a direct comparison, but it seemed to Easten they were travelling at a more relaxed pace. It could also be there was less frenetic urgency or fear of pursuit: he had no doubt the hodgepodge of disorganised pursuers they glimpsed briefly before entering the untamed forest would not have made much headway, assuming they had dared to chance passage of the pathless wilderness. He now had the luxury of being able to look back, confident his mount would not stumble on the flat, even ground. The forest that had allowed them to pass unhindered (and appeared to have sealed the passage as soon as they passed) was already some distance, an unbroken solid screen of foliage, dark in the distance and somehow forbidding. There was no sense of danger or pursuit, and he sensed no fear of possible pursuit from that direction.

CHAPTER TEN

Once Sí and her brothers had refreshed in the river, Palle and Easten had covered a significant distance along the bank. The forest was a vague blue-green blur covering most of the eastern horizon, and the river was turning into a wetland which would eventually become a lake.

When the five sprites were on the road again, they were energised from their immersion, and their speed increased. Soon the scenery was flashing past Easten's eyes as before, though his nerves and muscles insisted they were making no more than a light canter on the road.

The river/wetland went swiftly from an amorphous semi-solid state to a point at which it could definitely be defined as a lake, with a clearly delineated shoreline. Easten reined in as they approached the southernmost tip of the lake. There was no obvious path, no way to tell if there was any advantage in circling the lake with or against the clock.

He gazed at the lake, his attention snagged by a series of shapes, too regular to be natural, at the extreme edge of his vision, as far along the western bank as he could see with certainty. He was aware of Sí standing at his shoulder, waiting patiently.

"We are far from our own lands, and the only counsel I can give you now is this. As a water sprite I can tell you that the path that follows the western shoreline is firmer, easier for travel on two feet or four: I sense there is traffic on the road that way, and the path running east of the lake is longer as well as in a poorer condition. But if you are more concerned with preserving the secrecy of your travel, that would be the logical choice."

"No, that I cannot countenance!" Easten exclaimed. "I refuse to sneak into the lodgings of my master's kin like a thief in the night, skulking from every ragamuffin child! I will present myself and my companion at the main gate as befits the message my liege lord has required me deliver! As you reminded me when we met, there is the matter of my lord's honour that must be satisfied!"

"There's fire in the man, too!" Sí exclaimed, with a wide grin.

"That is what I most hoped to hear from you, my friend! I knew you had it in you to make the right decision, but it had to come from your heart, not any promptings of mine or my siblings."

She signalled her brothers, grouped at a discreet distance. Knowing how close they were, and their preference for mental communication, Easten was certain the hand gesture had been more for his convenience.

They lined themselves in a semi-formal ring, attentive to Easten. Sí gave him the gentlest prod in the right direction. "Our esteemed friend and bravest herald, Easten, has made his decision." Standing back, she left Easten alone on a miniature stage with a captive audience.

"I would not have managed the journey across Erin without your assistance. I had no call upon your services, and I am now deeply indebted to all of you. My colleague and fellow musician will accompany me on the last stage of my quest, on a public road that may present obstacles and difficulties, but your duty as escorts ends here. I would not ask you to place yourselves in danger…"

Sí interrupted. "You have not known us long and have little knowledge of our customs! You could not be expected to know of the *geas* that would befall us if we should look away, refusing to assist kin or a close friend such as yourself and your companion when they must face a difficult or dangerous situation in life!"

She rounded on her heel and addressed her brothers as if Easten and Palle were invisible, inaudible, or in an entirely different part of the country where they could play no part in discussions of the situation as she saw it.

"A message from a true prince of men in Cymru should be delivered to his brother, High King Cormac Rú of Tara, in a fitting and honourable manner. His envoy, Easten, fondly imagines he can achieve this with no more ceremony than he can conjure from his presence, together with his companion Palle and the quality of the music of his lute, Perori. But such a regal envoy deserves due honour and respect, and whatever escort can be provided. Easten would absolve us from further escort duties…" She paused and choked out a brief spatter of humourless laughter. "But I say, if we walk now, we are not honouring the man, the mission, or the faraway liege lord whose future, safety, even life, may depend on the success or failure of our friend Easten's long journey!

"Few we may be, but no envoy or ambassador can claim to have been escorted to the High King of Tara, who sits on the highest throne in the land, by an honour guard of the Fianna!"

She whirled once more on her heel. "Easten, you have said you will take the High Road, and I applaud your decision! But I cannot allow you to take it alone, not after the adventures we have shared, travelling the land from Dubh Lyn to Carraig with your liege lord's request. That is not the way of the Færy race, not in any of the world's la…" She cut herself off midword and reddened, as swiftly and as uncontrollably as a young child caught in a petty indiscretion by the world's strictest grandparent.

She glared at Easten for two or three eternal seconds before growling: "See what happens when I lose control of my tongue! Now, unless I have your sworn oath you will never, ever reveal to anyone the fact that the Fianna live side by side with Mortal communities throughout the known world, I will be forced to ensorcel you, either by making it impossible for you remember the fact you 'almost' heard from my unguarded lips or by placing a physical block on your tongue, and you will be unable to speak on this or any other subject for the rest of your life. I imagine that would be the worst fate for any troubadour, poet or musician!"

Easten had the grace to acknowledge the tone of rebuke in Sí's voice, whether he deserved it or not. "You have trusted me, a stranger you met by on the road, and granted a swift and secure passage to my destination. I hope I may show we Mortals are as trustworthy as the noblest Færy folk, the *Shii*, and the Fianna—whatever term they use to refer to themselves, wherever they may be found! What man with the least semblance of honour could take advantage of a moment's unguarded vigilance and betray another's trusted secret? I can only give my word and must hope you will accept it at its face value."

Sí glanced briefly at her siblings, who had not moved from the 'honour guard' position they had taken when summonsed. This time, Easten felt a curious feathery tingle caress a spot deep within his mind as the four brothers raised their heads and locked eyes on their sister. Was he becoming closer to the Fianna, sensing the contact between them? And if this were the case, could he hope... Sí ended her brief consultation with the brothers and stared at Easten with an odd blend of emotions in her eyes, face, even her body posture.

"I am aware you truly sensed something as I conferred with my brothers—though I am also certain you had no intention of prying! But you should know, in all the long years of my life in the Fianna, I have never met or heard of a Mortal who was closely attuned to us as anything more than the stuff of legend and folk tale and certainly not one sensitive enough to be able to 'feel' the connection between two or more of our number. There is more to you than meets the eye!"

"Yet I had no thought to... intrude in any way!" Easten was quick to assure.

Sí raised one hand in conciliation and agreement.

"Easten, I consider it my honour to bestow on you the title of friend, one earned on merit. We of the Fianna do not bestow titles lightly and especially not on short-lived Mortals, who are by our reckoning of the years recent shoots on one branch of a sapling tree on the edge of a Great Woods, now ready to produce its first crop of fruit.

"I sensed that you had somehow felt something at the moment my siblings and I held a brief conference. Believe me, I was just as surprised as you! In the years I have studied and read all I could find about our race history and traditions I have never come across any hint of such a thing before."

"I have no words to describe what I 'felt'…" Easten murmured, racking his brain and poet's soul for adequate vocabulary before the memory faded forever.

Sí smiled once more; the patient, warm smile a mother bestows on a well-loved child. "You have seen a mere thirty or so summers come and go Easten, while even my youngest brother, Four…" she indicated one of the siblings with a flap of one hand "…has seen ten times that number of winters! So, when I say that I as Firstborn have never known any Mortal coming close to what you achieved today, without conscious effort, I believe we have all been privileged to witness a unique moment in the relationship between two of the races who populate this world."

"You said: 'Two of the races…'" Easten murmured. "Does that mean there are more, the Mortal and the Færy? Why have I not heard more of the existence of other races except in tales told by troubadours, or recited to small children by elderly aunts and grandmothers?"

"Ah, once more the quick mind of the Mortal picks the most telling question! Yet since you ask, Easten, I will attempt to answer as truthfully as I may, though I cannot be certain that all I have read or heard from wiser, older heads than mine is true!"

"Before we met, my study of ballads and song had led me to believe the Fianna were also an invention…" Easten retorted, warming to the prospect of a keen exchange of arguments, a pastime he rarely had chance to enjoy unless his work travelling to deliver messages at Lord Caradoc's behest took him to one or other manor of the most important lords who ruled as large a portion of the Welsh Marches as they could control.

Sí nodded. "You have a quick wit to match your argument!"

"Yet the tally of races that live or have lived on this planet may not be known with absolute certainty. We have the tales of the Færy (and all the names associated with their kind), and you have the recorded history of Mortals. Both include records of a wide variety of creatures with different names. The one thing they have in common is a tendency towards Evil, a Darker Nature; creatures to be feared and avoided whenever possible!"

"Is it possible tales of monsters, giants, ogres and other dread creatures may be based on reality, not just figments of a poet's imagination?" Easten cried. The hairs rose on the back of his neck as a nightmare painted itself in a dark corner of his imagination and refused to be expunged.

Sí inclined her head once more.

"You yourself must have heard the phrase, that there is 'many a tune may be played on an old fiddle'? And have you never considered the same might also be said of some of the ancient folk tales, embedded in memories from before the time writing became a more permanent method of preserving the tales told around campfires when Mortals rose above other forms of animal life?"

Easten had no ready reply, but Sí looked sharply at one of her siblings; Easten had to assume that her brother (Easten thought it might be the youngest, Four) had lobbed her a mental note. After a short, silent exchange of stares Sí nodded to her sibling. Easten, watching intently, was certain he had spotted the slightest flicker in the brother's eyes, as if an inner light had been snuffed when contact was broken. He looked at Sí and found himself already under her scrutiny.

"I believe I also felt your 'presence' for a moment that time, my friend! I'm glad I had already made the decision to accept you as you are, and I value your friendship. Such sincere people as yourself are not often or easily met in life!"

She eased herself round to stand by Easten's side and address the group. "We have come this far as escort and honour guard on your journey, Easten. I will not countenance any suggestion we stand aside. That would be churlish, a mockery of the honour your entry to the High King's court merits and deserves!

"We must make our way to Cormac's residence with all the pomp and ceremony we can muster: I am certain you will be the first to present himself at Trinity Isle, where the High King holds court, in the company of a full set of the Fianna as his personal Honour Guard!"

Easten and Palle led their horses to a convenient bend in the river, where they were allowed to drink and had all the burrs and dust brushed out of their coats. When the grooming was complete, the horses gleamed and sparkled in the afternoon sun.

Before mounting, Easten decided Perori's significance, so central to the mission's success, deserved to be brought to the fore. It was time she was unpacked and paraded with deference and honour. She had been silent through their journey from Dubh Lyn, but as soon as he stripped away the layers of protective silks and leather cocooning her, she sighed a simple chord of surpassing beauty, the mark of a living, breathing independent entity, surfacing after a long refreshing sleep.

He handed the lute to Palle to use both hands getting into the saddle.

He was accustomed to controlling the horse with his knees and thighs, leaving his hands free to strum and experiment with familiar and original melodies while travelling long and often solitary roads on Lord Caradoc's business.

Palle stood close to Easten's left stirrup cup, waiting until his companion was ready for Perori to be delivered into the crook of his arms. As always, she was in tune, though she had been packed and unplayed for days. She felt warm, even physically desirable, and when Easten indicated he was ready to receive her Palle felt a strange, selfish reluctance to relinquish her to her rightful owner. Common sense and good manners combined to overcome these unexpected and out-of-character subsurface feelings for an object of intense beauty and mystery, which he knew was not his to covet.

Sí chose to stride at the head of their procession, with Easten and Palle riding side by side in the centre of a diamond formed by her brothers. The road that unrolled before them along the western bank of Lough Cé was firm and smooth. To begin they had it to themselves, but word of their progress was evidently spreading. More and more people gathered on both sides of the road to observe and evaluate the formal march of seven strangers and one musical instrument heading for the court of the High King, for a purpose they could only speculate.

The lake was dotted with several islands of various sizes. Some barely more than a few stones, barren and ungrassed, hardly worthy of the name. Others equally clearly settled. Houses and larger buildings visible from the shoreline, many with smoke billowing from roof vents and other signs of occupation.

The general shape of the lane bent slightly to the north, but the northern end of the lake was too far away to be clearly visible, and hidden from their position on the western bank by the positioning of the inhabited larger islands.

They rounded another bend and came to a bay where a sturdy wooden jetty had been built. Two of the largest islands Easten had seen on this final stage of their journey were close to the shore. The jetty was clearly there for the convenience of the residents on one or both islands.

The five-strong escort of Fianna, diamond-lozenged around a pair of brightly gleaming stallions, was an imposing display as they marched into the village proper, but it was Perori, sparkling as if inlaid with tiny diamonds from stem to belly, who drew the attention of every eye as they neared the village square and central jetty. Every child took the opportunity to tag along behind the rearguard, forming a ragged and cheerful (if untidy) tail to the procession.

"I sense that this is as far as we will travel—at least, for the moment!—on this road!" Easten commented, drily. The swelling crowd of bystanders had not confined themselves to flanking the road, but had spilled into the roadway while leaving open the option of making a right turn onto the jetty, as if they assumed this to be their intended destination.

Sí slowed her stride to drop to Easten's side for a private word as they turned onto the jetty. "I told you Cormac Rú has his residence in a fortified castle on Trinity Isle. As you can see, it is not far from the shore, but being on an island does make for an extra natural defence against surprise attack!"

"But to reach the High King, we must first persuade the ferryman to transport us, and that might not be so easy!"

It was on the tip of Easten's tongue to ask Sí to explain herself more fully, but a swift nod from her directed his attention to a pair of rough-dressed, middle-aged men at the end of the pier. They appeared not to be giving the visiting entourage their undivided attention. In truth, they appeared to have no interest or concern for anyone other than themselves. They stood as close as two people can without leaning on each other. Easten's first thought was that the only reason they were not already at each other's throats was that each one couldn't bear the thought of touching their opponent. There was barely an inch of clear air between their chests, their heads were thrust even further forwards, their faces red, spittle flew from each into the other's face, and both were screaming non-stop, seemingly oblivious to whatever the other said.

"It seems our first problem is going to be separating the two ferrymen without becoming involved in a minor war, or worse!"

Easten and Palle exchanged a concerned glance, then dismounted and hitched their mounts to a convenient post. From its height and positioning, it was probably intended as a mooring point for a small dinghy, but there was a slight area of grass within reach for the horses to graze on.

Easten cradled Perori securely as they strolled the jetty's length. Before they reached the half distance, he felt the lute vibrate against his arm, to emit a plaintive, distressed minor chord—or more accurately, he amended, a unpleasant, random jangle, a discord. Instantly, the war of words ceased, both protagonists halting mid-scream and at the same moment. If it hadn't been for the fact that the situation was so clearly escalating towards an imminent and violent physical altercation, the abrupt halt might have been comical. For a long moment, silence hung; the tension was almost palpable.

Nobody moved, indeed, it seemed nobody dared breathe. Easten knew he hadn't moved the fingers of his left hand that cradled Perori's neck (though he might have tightened the muscles in his fingers automatically and without thought). He was equally certain neither he nor Palle had (even by accident) brushed a hand over her belly, strumming her strings: but somehow, and in contrast to the harsh jangle ground out of the depths of her soundbox scant seconds before, a series of pure honeysweet melodic chords took flight, starting as a whisper, expanding rapidly until it seemed no other sound in Nature could compete. If musical signs (or even small animals representing musical notes) had appeared in mid-air, dancing in time to the music, Easten didn't think he'd have been too surprised.

The warring brothers straightened from their forward-hunched, threatening stance; each took a half-step back and looked the other in the eye before stepping closer. Each was now set on being the first to offer his hand in reconciliation, complicated by the fact each also tried to insist the other was blameless, and that "he" (alone) was entirely responsible for the 'misunderstanding' that was the sole reason for them almost coming to blows. Easten guided his honour guard to the end of the jetty with a measured, purposeful stride he hoped would be impressive without appearing menacing. The newly reconciled mortal enemies faced the party with deferential smiles of welcome and a brotherly arm around each other's shoulder.

Whether by accident or design, Easten's fingers brushed Perori's strings as he bowed to greet the ex-pugilists, releasing another shower of living musical notes that lingered on the still air, delighting the ear, enhancing everything it touched. The colour of the leaves and the scent of flowers might never have existed prior to being created this moment by the magic of the music. Everything had that indefinable, yet unmistakeable feel of original, fresh new creation; even the air filling Easten's lungs had a flavour, an almost intoxicating zest.

"I require transport, that I may seek audience with High King Cormac Rú, and lay a petition from my liege lord and his brother, Caradoc. His business is private and urgent, and I will require both your vessels to accommodate my retinue to Trinity Isle. Will you accept the charter? I can promise you both whatever fee or fare you name."

The brothers had no hesitation in returning Easten's bow and stood aside in mirror symmetry to allow the party to divide between the ferries nestling at the end of a short flight of steps. Easten sat on the broad rear bench and indicated Palle join him.

Sí raised a cautionary finger. "A moment, friend Palle! Allow me to step into the vessel first, lest it tip from lack of balance!"

With the practiced ease that can only come from years of living on and around rivers, lakes and the range of vessels that move people and goods each day by water she stepped into the narrow half seat at the bows before nodding to indicate it was safe for Palle.

"It is clear, neither of you are attuned to life afloat!" she said, with a disarming smile.

"I beg to differ, Milady!" Palle protested. "How can you think that of one who has sailed…"

"Yes, my point exactly!" Sí interrupted.

"You said, 'sailed'. Sailing is something an experienced mariner may do in a large, stable longboat. Such vessels are broad in the beam, sturdy, well balanced to cope with high seas and inclement weather! I don't need to risk my life on such vessels to know there is a world of difference in the skilful handling required to scull a smaller craft such as these against the currents of a fast river, or the freezing depths of a lake as large as Lough Cé!"

"You are well advised by this young lady!" came a pleasant lilting voice from the quayside. Easten glanced sharply upwards: the movement was enough to set the boat rocking alarmingly, confirming Sí's warning.

"My name is Colm; my brother Podraig and I will be honoured to provide the transport you require to complete the last stage of your journey. I hear from your accent your home lies far from Tara, and yet I hear you speak the Gael, even if certain words sound strange, as if your very throat and tongue are not familiar with the words they are asked to…"

An odd, slightly petulant and harsh scrape emanated unbidden from Perori's depths. Easten realised he had been 'hearing' Colm's words through the still-unexplained instant translation she supplied, and which he had now come to accept as a 'normal' communication tool. The final word of the sentence was omitted, almost as if it was impossible to translate, even for Perori's unique talents.

Easten was certain he understood the general idea, and let it pass.

It took seconds for Sí's five siblings to load themselves into the second skiff, distributing their not inconsiderable bulk and combined weight evenly and without disturbing the craft's equilibrium—in fact, barely causing it to bob on the lake's mirror-calm surface. Sí was watching Easten's expression as they settled quickly and efficiently. Her childlike laughter broke into his thoughts.

"Fear not! I need but a few more days travelling alongside you and I can teach you enough to be sure you can be trusted not to drown yourselves every time you cross a stream!"

She unhitched the painter that secured the bows to the pier as she spoke, and Colm plied his oars smoothly and powerfully to carry them out towards the largest island, which also happened to be the one closest to the shoreline.

Although they had not attempted to send any signal by flag, semaphore or other means, they arrived at the corresponding pier to an ordered detail of liveried staff who bowed deeply as Colm assisted his 'landlubber' passengers from their seats to the bank. Sí and her brothers had no need of this small courtesy, but that didn't prevent Podraig making the offer, or bowing his thanks for being allowed to carry them across the lake.

A note was sounded by an invisible musician inside the castle. Easten's ear identified it as a horn, one of the smaller instruments, pitched higher than most. A long series of notes reached out to welcome them, as they reached the main gates and Perori responded with a majestic peal, sounding for all the world like the chuckling of an innocent young child.

Sentries at the gate presented arms as the massive wooden doors eased silently open to admit them, and servants were immediately on hand to offer scented water and hot towels to remove the dust of the journey. A liveried page stood with a salver in his hands. Easten placed on it a leather pouch Palle had noticed without paying it special attention. It has been secured to one of the shrouds and covers used to protect Perori from damage and weather along the way, and Palle had assumed it contained a few accessories and spare parts.

Easten noticed Palle's speculative glance and grinned. "Where's the best place to hide a tree? In a forest, yes? So if you have an important document and wish it to remain secret, sometimes the answer is to hide it in plain sight! That pouch contains the formal written request from my liege to his brother the High King. Once we have taken refreshment, I will beg audience and make any further explanation Cormac Rú may require once he has read his brother's petition."

A table had been prepared covered with cut meats and cheeses, and a variety of breads, most beyond Easten's experience despite his travelling to all parts of Caradoc's domain and those of neighbouring barons. Carafes of wine had been placed at one end of the table, with appropriately sized gold and silver goblets grouped around them. At the opposite end of the table were two unlabelled bottles and half a dozen glasses holding no more than a single swallow of liquid: perhaps a tenth the size of the wine goblets. Palle laid his hand on Easten's arm.

"I can tell you this much as a friend, and I sincerely

hope you will take no offence from my warning! I was served this drink several times during my first brief stay in Erin, and I can assure you there is a good reason for the glasses being so small! The drink is not a simple wine, despite its innocuous lack of colour or any strong aroma. It is potent, and every family is likely to have its own jealously guarded secret recipe. It is invariably made at home!

"We have a similar drink in my homeland: *brændevin*, or 'burnt wine' because we distil first the wine, then set it over the fire for a second burning, turning it into a more concentrated drink. It takes little to turn a man's head! Here it is called *poteen*, and it is a form of sport for these people to offer it freely to guests who have no previous knowledge of the drink, watching to see how much it takes before they fall over, drunk out of their wits! I will, however, say this much: once the victim has recovered, they are treated with all the deference, courtesy, and hospitality anyone could wish to receive. These people are fond of practical jokes, but they are amongst the friendliest, most hospitable folk I have ever had dealings with!"

Forewarned, Easten accepted a small measure of the clear liquid from Palle. Held against the sunlight that streamed from an upper window, it was slightly oily, with a tendency to cling to the inner surface of the glass when he shook it experimentally. His nose told him there was a vague suggestion of herbs infused in the drink, but the scent was not strong enough to identify what.

Taking the smallest sip, he held the *poteen* in his mouth to test the flavour on tongue and gums and felt his tastebuds explode. He thought of the fire-eaters he had seen time to time with a travelling troupe and circus entertainers. What he was experiencing had to be similar to swallowing real, living flames. His mouth sagged in surprise: automatically, he swallowed the spirit, along with the copious spittle his glands were now working overtime to produce in a futile attempt to extinguish the fire burning in his mouth and at the back of his throat. The warmth he felt seconds later was comfortable and far from unpleasant: he could feel the passage of this minute sip every inch as it observed the unbreakable natural rules of gravity and progressed from throat via the usual passage to his stomach, spreading a warm glow (or so it seemed) to everything it touched. His vision blurred, rubbing at his eyes with the back of his free hand, he was startled when he discovered it came away damp.

"That brought tears to your eyes!" Palle howled with satisfaction as he saw the look on Easten's face, an odd mixture of bemusement and shock as the *poteen* continued to course through his body, warming every part of him. This, he thought, must be what people mean when they say something is strong enough to make your toes curl. He suspected that the matted thatch of unruly hair on his head was rapidly curling into ringlets.

"It is certainly the most potent of drinks: I've never tasted anything even remotely like it!" he agreed "...and you were right to offer caution before I sipped; a careless swallow could easily have choked me! But the taste is pleasant, all the same. Do you know if one is supposed to add a measure of water or possibly another liquid, to temper the ferocity, the burning..."

"There's many would say what you're suggesting should be considered a crime!"

The comment came from another who had entered the room and approached them, flanked by two young boys in servant dress. There was more than a hint of irrepressible amusement in the voice, and no hint of malice. Easten placed his glass on the corner of the nearest table, to free both hands for a formal greeting. This was without question their host, Cormac Rú, a near-identical (but larger) version of Caradoc.

Cormac stopped at the spread of refreshments and poured wine into three goblets, measuring small tots of the fiery spirit into three clean glasses before indicating with a courteous gesture for Easten and Palle to join him on comfortable seating placed close to an open range where a healthy fire burned almost smokeless, fed by rough squares of dried turf rather than the split logs Easten was accustomed to on his travels around Cymru.

Cormac regarded his guests with an open, easy smile, raising the small glass in his right hand to propose a formal toast in welcome before they sat. "*Sláinte!*"

"*Slán leat!* Easten responded, automatically, and knew (without knowing how) that the slight difference in the words were not only 'right', but he was also just as certain Cormac had set a small test for him, one he had passed.

Cormac's eyes glowed with approval. "It would be difficult for me to keep my secrets hidden from you, Sire! I suspect the person my brother has sent as his envoy to my court is a man with more talents than those of a simple musician, however talented you are! I speak your tongue as well as my brother Caradoc, and for our convenience we can conduct what business may be necessary in that language, if that is more convenient! Are all my brother's staff such fluent linguists? From my own experience in the first years I came here, I know Gael is not the easiest language for one not born to it."

Again, Easten was obliged to recount for another listener the abbreviated version of how Perori's powers extended beyond the merely musical. Cormac made no attempt to interrupt, and had no questions when Easten concluded his account but nodded his acceptance of the tale without demands for proof.

"And you say you have a tradition in Cymru, to give an exceptional instrument the honour of a Name, as if it were a living, breathing, independent entity or creature with its own personality?"

"That is indeed true. I cannot be certain how far back the tradition stretches, but before the earliest written records. And 'Perori', as I said, means 'Music'."

"And in the Gael, that would be *'ceol'*." Cormac nodded. "A pleasant sounding word, and easy to remember! Your tradition has much to commend it, as a way of honouring an object that is rare, beautiful, maybe even… magical?"

"There are legends in which it is also said Kings and Princes have been known to honour a sword or another favoured weapon in similar fashion, My Lord: I have even heard tell of a King who enjoyed a cut of meat so much, he dubbed it "Sir Loin", if it please you to believe it or not!"

Cormac's eyes flashed to the viands on the side table for a moment before he looked back at Easten and roared with laughter. "Whether 'tis true or not, it makes a good tale, and I am now certain my brother is well entertained during the long winter nights in his draughty mausoleum, that pile of granite overlooking endless boglands in

Cymru! Why anyone would think them worth fighting over is a mystery to me, but I gather you are here on Caradoc's behalf to ask for my assistance, to support my young brother in defending his lands against an aggressor who would take by force what does not belong to him."

"In short, Sire, that's the very rub of it," Easten replied, bowing his head as he spoke. He felt certain Cormac was one who could be depended on to do what he believed right and honourable, but he wished he had taken more time to understand the ethics of the inhabitants of Erin, the way they thought, what they held to be important to their daily existence.

"You have been with my brother some time, I gather?"

Easten started but managed to keep his voice even. "Sire, I have had the honour to be at Caradoc's court for nigh on a decade."

"Musician, if you will consent to allow me to address you by your name, I believe our negotiations will move at a faster pace if we may dispense with titles—but only when we are alone! Here's my hand on it: do you agree?"

With barely a flicker of hesitation and a glance at his companion, Easten accepted Cormac's proposal. With the High King's tacit consent, Palle's hand overlaid both of theirs and he was awarded the same intimate courtesy.

"Convince me now of the reason (or reasons!) I should travel such a distance with a fighting force, risking attacks on the road, storms, fierce dragons and the dreaded *mal de mer* as we cross a short but nasty sea and several months away from wives, wenches and pretty colleens, to help my little brother out of a little local difficulty? I might even return home to find the Kingdom of Tara has been usurped by another! What ground can you give to persuade me to help him?"

Everything had been going well up to this point, Easten felt almost as if Cormac was toying with him. He leapt to his feet, an angry retort on his lips.

Cormac raised both hands in a placatory gesture. "Peace, Easten! Do not be so hasty to judge another! I am not under any duress, and I have good neighbours: the risk of an attack if I choose to be absent for any length of time is remote—but I needed to test how serious the situation is, before I decide! Your reaction tells me all I needed to know; I do not doubt but that you are a loyal and devoted aide and follower, and my brother is a fortunate man to have someone such as yourself to call upon.

"You may set your mind at ease! Blood, as we say, is thicker than water, and my men have been muttering about the lack of any challenge or excitement, no battles other than training exercises where the *coup de grace* must always be withheld, no heads to crack, not so much as a decent game of hurley as a poor substitute for warfare: they think we are in danger of becoming accustomed to an easy life!

"They will follow where I lead, and I now choose freely to lead them as swiftly as possible from Ros Comyn to Dubh Lyn, thence by sea to the bogs of Cymru and my beleaguered little brother. Are you content?"

The speed of Cormac's decision took Easten by surprise. He'd been expecting at the least a few days' delay while the High King took advice from a bevy of court officials, neighbours and a rag-tag of minor princelings before announcing his decision. Easten was on his feet without ceremony and had to restrain himself from throwing his arms around Cormac to express his thanks (even though there were no witnesses). Cormac was less concerned about protocol and didn't hesitate to sweep Easten and Palle into his arms in a three-way bearhug.

"Now that's decided, we still have a serious matter to discuss," he said, soberly. He went back to the serving table, returning with carafes containing all the remaining wine. He filled all three goblets to the brim before serving his guests and fixing a steely glare on Easten. "Now you can tell me how in all the Seven Ancient Kingdoms two travellers can arrive at the court of the High King himself with no less an Honour Guard than five—five!—of the Fianna in attendance?"

CHAPTER ELEVEN

"I had always thought the *Fianna* were legend, a tale from the very birth of time!"

"Yet here we are, as you see. We are indeed in this world, just as much as you. But the difference is this, we are not (and have perhaps never truly been) of it in the way you are.

"And as far as legends are concerned, we of the Fianna are long lived by your tally of the seasons. My brothers and I have kept a watchful eye on this world through more than four hundred winters. Does that make us legends—or a genuine part of recorded history? Do I appear a memory from bygone days?"

Sí's voice had taken on a shrill overtone and drew a sympathetic sigh from Perori's strings (though again, Easten was certain he had not touched them).

Disbelief, possibly tinged with alarm, crossed Cormac's face. "Tell me, Easten, does your wondrous Perori often show her feelings, her emotions, in this manner? Is it possible? Could she really be 'alive' in the full sense, an independent, thinking creature with a ... personality, able to express an opinion?"

"If I am honest, High King—for honest I must be!—I have thought on this often over the years, particularly on this most recent of my travels to date! She has on many occasions proved—to me, at least—that she can exert a calming influence if we find ourselves in or close to a scene where conflict is present or seems likely to develop. This has happened times without number, and since we were so fortunate to meet this family group of Fianna her tendency to encourage peace and goodwill has become ever easier to recognise!"

Without making any conscious decision Easten found he had eased Perori from a 'port' position to the one he preferred for storytelling. He strummed softly two or three times while he pondered his next move and extemporised a new melody with his fingers, as his voice told in a pleasant, clear baritone their meeting with the five siblings at the river marking the boundary of Dubh Lyn's jurisdiction. Easten had not planned this, and had no idea what the next line of the song might prove to be. He let the words tumble from his lips and spread to all sides. Several kitchen and other staff had gathered unaccountably, entranced by the beautiful, compelling music.

The chords grew in volume, filling the room, calling forth a bass rumble from the timbered wall mountings, setting the flames in the wall sconces to dance with a fresh vigour.

Easten felt curiously detached, an invisible observer watching the performance without comment or judgement. Even though he knew he was the performer, plucking and strumming the accompaniment to the tale being told through his lips, he was somehow at one and the same time positioned slightly off to one side, looking over his own left shoulder from about six feet behind and slightly above, the point of view of a small giant standing on a stairwell.

It was a strange experience, seeing and hearing himself sing. The sound was not distorted, his fine-tuned musician's ear told him, and there was a slight (but definite) 'lag', as if the words and music were delayed, coming a fraction of a second later than expected.

He listened intently as the ballad told of the seemingly chance encounter between himself, Palle and Perori with Sí and her brothers, and an account of their journey from Dubh Lin to Tara's Halls. Extravagant praises of High King Cormac Rú were woven into the later stanzas, and it struck Easten as remarkable that 'he' (the singer, not the listener) could have known enough about the King's life and deeds to extemporise such a magnificent, detailed pæn of praise without an opportunity to sit in a quiet corner with a handful of quills and make several pages of notes before daring to perform even a short epic ballad for the person to whom it was dedicated.

The final verse spoke of the purpose of Easten's long journey from Cymru and ended with Caradoc's impassioned plea for assistance from his brother.

Easten closed his eyes briefly as the final chord hung in the air. When he opened them a second later, he discovered he was 'back' to seeing the world from his accustomed perspective, with Perori nestled in his arms once more.

A contemplative silence settled on the chamber: Cormac appeared deep in thought: Easten felt it would be the height of ill manners to presume to speak before the King, and used the opportunity to ponder the lyrics he had just heard himself sing, asking himself how he could possibly have composed such powerful verses without days or even weeks of preparation and study.

Cormac stirred. "Easten, I thank you for these words, they are far beyond any I have ever heard sung, even for our greatest heroes of legend! I will try to live up to the noble portrait you have painted of me, but it will be no easy task!

"There is one thing I fail to understand. How did you have time to write such beautiful words, such thrilling and exciting music, in the brief time you have spent in our country, and most of that travelling the long and sometimes perilous road between Dubh Lin and this region of Tara? You have scarcely had time to ride here at full gallop, and without stopping, yet you have somehow managed a composition! How can that be? And for the second, I was not aware that the adventures and exploits of my family—and my own part in the clan records!—were common knowledge more than a day's ride in any direction. Where did you obtain such detailed information?"

Easten began to make a formal bow before replying, but Cormac tutted and with a wave of his hand indicated he should return to the informal group of padded seats they had been sitting in before he had delivered Caradoc's request for assistance. He set Perori carefully on her stand before resuming his place.

"With your permission, my Lord…"

"Cormac: as I have already said, I value you and your superb musical instrument as personal friends! Being treated as royalty can sometimes be a tiresome and lonely existence. There are few who dare call me friend, probably for fear of jealousy. We should not be wasting time on formal titles!"

"As you wish… Cormac." Easten had clearly been on

the point of using a title again but caught himself. "If I may be so bold, however, I think I can answer the second question more easily than the first. Is that acceptable?"

Cormac nodded. Easten felt encouraged by his minor victory.

"Even to me this seems little more than a part answer, and far from satisfactory, but it is all I can offer. There is much I myself fail to understand! I cannot say how far the fame due the most powerful ruler of the Seven Kingdoms has carried, but I am certain that all who live and breathe in Erin must know something of the history of the ruling family in the largest and most powerful of them all, Tara.

"Until recently I was an ordinary Court Musician in a country separated from Erin by seas, which I am told can be dangerous even in the best weather. I was only made aware that there was a land to the north and west of the isle of Ynys Môn, the most northern part of Cymru, when your brother, my liege lord, set me the task of delivering to you his sincere greetings, one Clansman to another, and to beg for assistance he sorely needs.

"When we arrived in Dubh Lin..." Easten paused.

No! Surely that was not possible. One night they had slept in Dubh Lin, following the evening of entertainment and the discussions after the meal. He had a ready memory for maps, and could calculate distances, but even so, and allowing the possibility that their headlong westward 'Supergallop' had been real, not just a figment of his imagination, it was simply not possible they had achieved the journey in a single day, with neither rest nor even the shortest break for themselves and their horses... was it?

He had to continue his explanation, before Cormac

lost interest, or worse, began to suspect he was not being told all the facts. But how could he tell the High King—or anyone—the whole truth when he found it difficult to recall where he'd heard… whatever he thought he'd heard, or even who he'd heard it from?

"In Dubh Lin," he continued, "I discovered that Perori made it possible for us to understand the people we met, even though we spoke different languages—as we are doing now!"

"My ears tell me you speak my language as fluently as any in my family, yet my eyes tell me that your lips are forming words other than those I hear!" Cormac conceded.

"The same holds true for me… for us" Easten amended, glancing at Palle and receiving a nod. "But I think we must be grateful for the advantage we have from this gift of tongues. My lord Caradoc's situation grows more difficult with each day, and if I can persuade you to assist your brother with a show of arms, my journey home will be longer than the ten days since I left him."

"Simply reaching Tara from Dubh Lin in a single day tells me you have had some assistance of a magical nature already!" Cormac said, glancing at the honour guard of Færy figures who stood in silence at Easten's shoulder. Easten caught Sí's eye and gestured for her to step forwards.

"Palle Stormsinger and I met with our travel companions by chance (or so it seemed) on the road west of Dubh Lin. Once again, Perori mediated our understanding of each other, but on this occasion, it seemed we understood each other's thoughts, without the need to speak our needs. After we had shared a meal, they made it possible for us to outstrip a band who tried to pursue us. I am certain we could not have ridden so rapidly to Tara unaided."

Cormac nodded, turning slightly as if intending to address Sí directly.

Though Easten's hands were at rest cradling Perori, and he knew he hadn't accidentally brushed her strings, he felt her stir faintly in his arms as she breathed a soft but powerful chord, just loud enough to be heard. The expressions on every face told him that he was not alone in hearing it.

A total silence settled on the room. Easten felt the tensions building almost unnoticed within his consciousness throughout this interview eased, as if magically wiped away by a caring mother's soft hands. He discovered he had to make a conscious effort to flex the muscles in his neck to look around the room: time slowed as he registered every detail of each person's features and clothing, the veneer of the furniture, the colour of the fabrics, the quality of the sunlight refracting through the glass in the windows high on the end wall.

Somehow, he knew Sí was holding a silent (very private) conversation with Cormac. Perhaps it was an intimate melding of minds, like several occasions he'd noticed during their wild gallop when she'd 'spoken' to one or more of her brothers. It neither frightened him, nor was he surprised. These were Færy folk: why would they not have their own ways of communicating?

It was evident from the unfocussed gaze on the faces of all present that they were also at peace, and no more aware of the private conversation between the High King and the Færy Queen than he was. To him, this was logical, fair, reasonable. Kings and the Fae were of a different ilk than ordinary folk.

"Do not demean your talents, Easten! The true nature of your special Gift will be revealed to you and those around you, all in good time!"

The mild reproof, delivered in Sí's familiar Voice without her turning to face him or moving her lips, formed as a full, instant thought. Nobody else reacted, and Easten knew—again, without understanding how or why—that this remark had been addressed to him, and him alone. With a barely perceptible fraction of a nod he accepted the gentle reprimand, and consciously tried to 'think' a wordless but sincere apology. Sí raised one hand (a token of acknowledgement,) and Easten's mind eased once more into a comfortable, warm state of unthinking oblivion. He assumed Sí was concluding her private interview of High King Cormac. The vague half-smiles in the room suggested he was not the only one enjoying a few moments luxurious relaxation in a private Nirvana.

It might have been the smallest gesture, or the least hint of a long-postponed breath. Easten knew Cormac had returned from wherever Si entrancelled him. He bowed formally, indicating that he was content to wait for Cormac to take the discussion in whichever direction he favoured.

"You have made a long and arduous journey to deliver my brother's petition, Bard Easten! Let me therefore set your mind at ease: I am not one to turn a deaf ear to a sibling or any family member who asks for help! You and your marvellous instrument pleaded his case with a grace and elegance that would have melted the hardest hearts, with the support of your travel companions." He nodded to Sí and her brothers, who had advanced to stand at her shoulders.

"In itself that is enough to tell me my brother's cause is just! They cannot be deceived by dissemblings: they rarely concern themselves with human affairs, and their decision to assist on your quest is all the confirmation I need!

"Sí has also told me this: she and her brothers have already decided they will accompany us as far as Dubh Lin. My forces will reach the ferry with all speed—and I shall lead them. I don't intend to give my brother the opportunity to deny me a good fight!"

"We have agreed to lead you on the same secret paths we used to come to Tamhair. Your army will arrive unmolested and unseen in the Danegeld you know as Dubh Lin."

As Easten digested this swift mental signal from Sí, Cormac turned his attention to the one member of the group who had been trying desperately to make himself inconspicuous. "Stand forth, Brion, and report to your Clan Chief! Have you repented of your decision to follow the new religion?"

"No, Sire! I am here courtesy of Bard Easten's invitation; he asked if I would assist with understanding the Gael, but that was before we discovered Perori's magical properties with languages... and in truth, I was glad of the chance he offered me to visit your court, this will always be my true home!"

Cormac smiled. "Your tongue has lost none of its powers to persuade, Brion! Have a care, lest I and others start to believe you speak the truth! Still, I concede you have always had a certain skill with languages, and I have no doubt you would have made yourself useful, but for the mystical powers invested in this unique instrument.

"All able-bodied riders will muster at sunset, bearing each his preferred weapons. We travel under the guidance and protection of the *Shii*, and ride through the night to reach Dubh Lin by daybreak We turn neither left nor right and will not pause for meals: our coming will be swift and silent. No food supplies, no extra baggage. We must reach my brother with all speed!"

CHAPTER TWELVE

Cormac Rú sat at ease on his preferred war horse on the palace forecourt. Over two hundred veterans were assembled, ready to ride into the night. The control they displayed was such, there was barely a jingle of war harness, or a nervous hoof scuffed against a cobblestone. The discipline of the men and their mounts was impressive.

A suitable horse had been found for Brion, who had the basics of riding.

Easten and Palle Stormsinger had been 'doubled' as passengers riding with two of Cormac's seasoned warriors.

As the sun dipped below the parapet and the shadows lengthened in the courtyard the main gates opened. Cormac Rú was limned as a giant silhouette halo'ed by a mane of red hair that seemed afire. He gazed with clear approval over the assembled ranks of straight rows of riders with complete control over their steeds. He straightened his knees, rising from his saddle, and unsheathed a great broadsword. As he flourished it above his head, the last rays of the setting sun coruscated along its full length, a living flame trailing sparks in its wake, singing a defiant song of challenge as it cleaved the air above his head.

"My brave Knights of Tamhair! We ride tonight to aid

my brother, across the seas to the east, who is sore pressed defending his lands! We ride under the shield and protection of the *Shii*, who have guaranteed a swift and secret passage by ways known to them alone. Even the wind will not keep pace with us this night, nor will our passage be noted by any human eyes or ears. We arrive in far off Dubh Lin by daybreak! Ride, now, Án Tamhair!"

The battle cry was repeated from the throat of every rider as Cormac Rú, Prince of Coolavin and High King of Tamhair, wheeled his mount and led his troops through the gate and into the gathering gloom. The five *Shii* flowed to form a silvery arrowhead, sweeping aside the shadows. For the first half dozen ranks of riders, the way ahead was as clear and easy to negotiate as if they were riding in a sun-drenched noon; those further back had only the man and horse in front of them as guide but trusted in that and settled swiftly into the same furious pace.

Palle and Easten were carried as non-combatant passengers on two horses in the leading phalanx. Palle felt a sharp but painless 'tug' at his mind and glanced to one side, knowing Easten was trying to get his attention. As their eyes locked. Palle heard Easten's voice inside his head. "Are you listening, my friend? Over two hundred horse—or eight hundred hoof, if you will—but not a murmur! And I suspect, if we could but see the ground over which we are passing, not so much as a blade of grass bent out of place!"

There was no way this could be verified, but Palle did not doubt Easten's words would prove true. He thought of his own doubts on the outward journey. On that occasion, he'd been wrong. They hadn't flown from Dubh Lin, westwards to Tamhair, but if his ears were believed it seemed they were now in every sense flying on the return journey.

Although the night was dark, with no moon and low, dense cloud cover, the darker shadow of a sprawling forest was easy to identify. Every rider sensed the same mental request ('command' would have been too strong) to reform the ranks from line abreast to a narrow double column. The vanguard of five Færy beacons closed to form a needle-thin arrowhead aiming at the closest point of the woods. As they reached the eaves, Easten realised they had climbed still further. They weren't going to ride through the woods: their escort clearly intended to lead them over the treetops.

With neither star nor discernible landmarks for guidance it was impossible for Easten to guess their speed, but before long he realised they had begun arcing back towards open ground beyond the forest. Soon they were galloping silently, scant inches above meadows of grass that bent, stirred by the close passage of the horses' hoofs. Untouched, unbruised, it wafted aloft a sweet perfume Easten could feel cleanse his senses. It sharpened his vision, enhanced his hearing, made the tips of his fingers super-sensitive: he had to fight an urge to remove Perori's protective wraps and play a new, wild, perfect melody into his conscious mind, inspired by the events of their headlong (but always perfectly controlled) flight without the need for clumsy, banal lyrics. The music was sufficient to describe the ride.

CHAPTER THIRTEEN

The bright five point of Færy light that guided them thus far faltered as they descended east of the dense, trackless wood. One of the four brothers, wide to the rear right flank of the riders, opened his throat and sounded a warning. The fear and alarm in the signal itself was sufficient, and everyone heard it clearly.

This time they did not check their descent a foot or two above the ground, as they had earlier in their sprint across Ros Comyn. The terrain was flat and even, but Easten distinctly felt the rumble of over eight hundred hoofs beat a regular tattoo against the ground. He glanced over his shoulder and wished he hadn't. The woods over which they had recently flown were only a few hundred yards away, but they were almost concealed behind a dense shadow that had either sprung or fallen from nowhere, without warning. Cormac was still at the head of his troops, his attention focused on the diminished energy displayed by their protective escorts. Every other rider was also giving their undivided attention to the unexpected developments ahead. As far as he could tell, Easten was the only one who had seen the imminent threat at their vulnerable rear.

In a flash he had Perori out of her protective wraps. Striking a firm chord, he felt her belly reverberate against his; her strings thrummed under his fingers, and the notes grew in strength and volume, an unmistakeable challenge to the mysterious, hidden adversary. Cormac stood in his stirrups and whipped his mount around on its hind legs.

His hand went over his head, using a signal that meant nothing to Easten but resulted in his followers executing a controlled halt. Within seconds they were regrouped in a fighting phalanx twelve across and ten deep. The speed and control this required dazzled Easten, who knew enough about horses to realise he understood nothing of the tactics or skills to fight from horseback.

Despite this, he could appreciate that such an unplanned manœuvre could only be successfully performed by well-trained troops.

He was now towards the rear of the field, just in front of the king, which gave him protection as a non-combatant. Without thinking, he continued to finger a series of chords and sang. The words were unimportant. The music sufficient: a series of crashing, challenging yet harmonious phrases of melody, unmistakably martial, frightening in power and volume, stirring any who fell under its spell with an undeniable lust for combat and victory. Their spirit world companions remained on the periphery: two on the left flank, three on the right, and towards the rear. They were clearly not preparing to join the imminent mêlée, opting to remain close as passive observers.

Cormac spurred his horse and galloped from the rear of the field brandishing the greatsword he pulled from its sheath, snug against his saddle. It was a true rider's blade, too long to be borne on a waistbelt or ceinture. It sparked with suppressed fury as he screamed a fearless challenge to the menacing shadow that advanced inexorably, obliterating every plant, bush and crevice, pooling and decanting its poison into every hollow it touched. A warrior of lesser stature would have needed both hands merely to carry such a weapon, but for Cormac it circled and flickered above his head, a deadly bejewelled toothpick with which the Clan Chieftain would slash the encroaching darkness into harmless tatters.

At the rear, Easten felt himself swept by the power of the music welling from Perori, growing in volume and intensity with every second. His fingers were a blur as he segued from one intricate chord to the next, the result wild and unbridled, inspiring the riders to challenge any force that dared confront them. The music was a vibrant, living entity, its beauty required no conscious effort, spreading like the ripples on a pond, which grew swiftly to waves, each more powerful than the one before, towering over the riders, a protective screen hovering—on the verge of being a visible shield. He felt the muscles of his throat constrict; it would burst if he did not add his voice to the complex challenge of the battlesong. He threw back his head and filled his lungs with air, the words which tumbled from his lips soared high, boosted and carried on Perori's music. His ears told him the language was one which he did not recognise, one he was certain he had never learned or even heard, but his brain insisted they were the only words to fit the anthem for troops poised to repulse the Darkness.

"A Tamhair!"

Cormac's voice carried even above the combined volume of Easten's song and Perori's music as he spurred his mount and led the charge. Although he had no memory of dismounting, Easten discovered he stood on a large, flat rock as the riders echoed Cormac's cry and swept away in tight formation, their swords unsheathed, glistening in the rays of the first light as the sun cleared the horizon behind them. Yet the music outstripped the fleetest horses; Easten saw clearly how the long grass and the bushes swayed and bent before the vanguard could lay hoof to it, flattened by the passage of an invisible but real physical presence ahead of the Clan Chieftain and his followers, protecting them from the encroaching cloud.

The music carried Easten's song higher and wider, increasing in intensity until it formed a near-visible hammerfist. The most advanced edges (wings? flanks?) of the unnatural opposing force wavered, then retreated. With a yell of triumph and a magnificent final cadence of achievement, the musical fist fell on the motionless shadow. All who witnessed the scene winced, anticipating an explosion, but there was none.

A commander in the vanguard later reported to Cormac, "To me it seemed the powerful fist of music flexed and opened to become the open palm of a giant's hand, which simply scooped the darkness from the land as cleanly as a skilled *chirugeon* excising rotten flesh from a wound in the hope of saving an injured man's arm. Seconds later, it rose again and closed into a fist, containing every scrap of the dark matter; as it squeezed tight once more, silent sparks and multi-coloured bolts of lightning shot from it and flew high into the sky, carried on the triumphant final tones of the music. The land that had been contaminated by the creeping malevolence regained its habitual colours, as if they had been called into existence for the first time. Fresher, and somehow healthier than my limited imagination or poor words could possibly describe!"

It had all happened so quickly; Cormac had not had time to consider what he had witnessed. As he mulled over his captain's report he glanced around, then frowned. "Where is the Bard, Easten? We are in sore need of his guidance!"

All eyes swivelled to the rear again, and a cry of alarm went up from those closest to the rock Easten and Perori had used as a podium. Cormac's view was obscured; he spurred his mount and galloped through the ranks.

Perori lay, apparently unscathed, cushioned on a large, leafy bush. The same could not be said of Easten, who lay pale and unconscious at the base of the rock. His companion, Palle knelt at his side, cradling the Bard's head. A young woman stood at his shoulder, bathing Easten's forehead with a cloth—probably whipped from her long russet mane of hair.

"Palle! What happened? Is he injured?"

Palle settled Easten's head in the girl's arms and rose. "Nobody saw him collapse, as far as I can tell, but Moirag was with a group of camp-followers who passed this way as the music reached its climax. They found him here, so pale they thought him dead. Yet he breathes—shallow and slow, but still! He is cold to the touch, and I am unable to awaken him." Moirag tugged at his sleeve and spoke rapid words. Palle nodded and turned back to the Clan Leader.

"Moirag begs permission to address *an MacDairmada* herself—she is a Healer, and I trust her judgement. She knows more of these things than I!" Cormac dismounted, pulling off his gauntlets as he approached in two or three swift strides. Moirag laid her patient's head on a folded cloak, placed her dampened headscarf across his forehead, and flowed gracefully to her feet when Cormac offered his hand.

"Sire, I find no sign of accident or injury; no wound on his body from dart or arrow, nor any cut from an enemy's sword. And his breath, though weak, is pure. He has not swallowed any poison I have learned about in my years of study as a Healer." She spoke clearly and humbly, but from behind an impenetrable veil of bright red hair, as if she dared not look directly at the Clan Chieftain until granted permission.

"Approach, Moirag! You are known to Palle, I understand! He has already shown his own skills in music: why would I not value your skills of healing?"

She tossed her hair back and made as if to kneel, but Cormac forestalled her with a light touch on the forearm and gazed deep into her eyes.

"We all have our special skills, and I sense that the Bard Easten needs yours now. What can you tell us? Can he be revived?"

She paused, rummaging blindly in a small cloth sac hanging from her belt. "I carry but a few simple herbs when we follow a camp, mostly those I need to stanch blood and heal wounds. His first needs are warmth and rest, and the benefits of other remedies I may have at home." She waved her arm vaguely to the east. "Can he be moved? There remains a half-hour's solid ride to Dubh Lyn!"

Moirag dropped to her knees and made a long, careful examination of Easten's still-comatose form. "He seems warmer, and I believe he breathes more easily…" She looked around, possibly searching for a particular plant or herb. As she gazed east she stopped. Her attention caught. She pointed, calling, "*An Trom!*"

Silhouetted against the skyline was the distinctive shape of a large tree standing clear as if in a clearing created for it. She turned to Cormac with excitement. "Sire, this tree is known for its range and potency of potions and charms. If we carry him there, I may be able to prepare something to help until he can be taken to a more suitable resting place!"

Six riders used shields as a makeshift pallet to carry Easten to the elder tree, about two hundred paces. When they arrived and Moirag saw a sturdy branch grew almost horizontal to the main trunk, starting just a few feet from the ground, she beamed with anticipation and had the shield-bearers place Easten on it. Palle was close. He had retrieved Perori from the lying bush and picked up the protective wrappings she would normally travel in but made no attempt to pack her. His first concern was to check for damage, but there was no indication of anything amiss. Had Easten some warning of a fit of faintness, and time to place the instrument carefully to one side? From the few clues, that seemed possible… Moirag looked up from her preparations and smiled at him; with a toss of her head she begged him to come closer. She had her hands full of berries, which Palle assumed she would press and crush to produce medicine. As she leaned on his shoulder to whisper a private word, a stray current of air soughed across the clearing. Perori's strings vibrated, resonating. The clear, sweet bellpeal was heard by everyone in the clearing. This time, instead of spreading like ripples on a pond they appeared to chase each other in a merry upward dance, twisting to a tight spiral, spinning around the bole of the tree, rising into the leafy canopy.

From somewhere in the folds of her skirt, Moirag produced a bowl and mashed the berries to a pulp. She stopped, cocking her head as if hearing a message she alone was privy to. She nodded and turned to Palle. "Place the instrument across his chest."

The litter-bearers had placed Easten on his back, feet against the bole of the tree: his arms dangled either side of the broad branch. Palle did as told, and as an afterthought placed Easten's arms across Perori, securing her in place. There was a suggestion of a muffled, melancholy mewl, damped to silence by the flaccid resistance of the Bard's unresponsive limbs.

Moirag continued to pound the berries, and soon had a small amount of liquid in the base of the bowl she decanted into a smaller container produced from a different part of her skirt, trying to avoid the seeds and fruit pulp from the base of the bowl.

"I may ask you to massage his throat, if I cannot rouse him and persuade him to drink this potion," she said to Palle, who nodded despite his incomprehension. Moirag added, "Swallowing is an instinct, but an unconscious patient will often shelter so deep from their ailment or injury they need assistance."

Palle's eyes glowed. He'd learnt something useful, without being made to seem an ignorant fool.

Easten's complexion had improved. He was no longer a waxy colour and his skin had texture. He as breathing more deeply, and with less obvious effort.

Moirag showed Palle how to provoke a 'swallow' reaction by stroking Easten's throat, relieved to note that the 'gag' reflex followed.

Silently she mimed to Palle that he should slide one hand behind Easten's head while she used a finger to separate his parched lips and poured a few drops of liquid into his mouth.

Three times she administered a thimble of liquid, watching carefully for any change in her patient. His skin regained a more natural tint, and his eyes blinked rapidly without quite opening. He stirred and twitched a little but was in no danger of falling from his improvised sickbed.

As Easten swam out of the murky depths, his fingers automatically sought their accustomed positions on the neck and belly of his beloved Perori. The upward angle of the branch he was lying on meant he was already in a semi-upright position: he played two or three experimental chords before he reached full awareness of his surroundings.

Moirag leant across Easten, pinning his shoulders, forcing him to relax.

"Stay where you are! I judge you too weak to move, and I am not yet finished with my healing!"

Without delay she did an intricate dance, crooning a wordless melody with raised her arms in supplication to *An Trom*, occasionally clicking her fingers to implore the ancient tree to lend its healing powers. As she concluded her prayer she sank gracefully against the tree roots, a picture of open, sincere obeisance.

"I feel much better now…" Easten began. Moirag rose to her feet.

"The potion I mixed for you will soon wear off; you must take solid food before anything else!"

Several people offered portions of soda bread, and Moirag broke a couple, soaking them in the scraps of fruit pulp in her mixing bowl.

"The fruits, leaves, flowers, even bark of the Elder tree all have different uses for a Healer," she informed Easten as she handed him the bread. "Unfortunately, the fruit itself has a bitter taste. I can only hope the bread will make it easier!"

It was late in the day. Easten was so hungry he'd have eaten anything, food or not. As he finished the final slice of bread, a cadre of warriors approached carrying a curious object, a slender triangular frame about eight or nine foot in length, lashed with rope.

"*Sínteàn!*" Moirag breathed. "Do you realise what this means? The men built this to carry you; the narrow end can be hitched to a horse, who will perform most of the hard work. Two or three men running on either side will prevent your falling, and we can make the harbour at Dubh Lyn in less than an hour. When we arrive, I will have more potions and remedies to aid your recovery!"

The stretcher might have been rapidly constructed, but it was solid, and Easten had no qualms allowing himself to be borne on it by half a dozen battle-hardened warriors—strangers who didn't even speak his language. It was harnessed to a large stallion in similar fashion to a simple farm plough and they set off at a brisk pace.

Easten didn't think he'd relax, but the effects of Moirag's potions wore off and he felt himself drifting. There was a cloud threatening to engulf his mind: he'd never felt so tired.

Palle and Moirag jogged easily ahead of the six stretcher-bearers, both with their eyes locked on the reluctant patient. Easten felt a warning tingle in his fingertips, and realised he was losing his grip on Perori.

He managed to raise a groan, and Palle signalled to the porters to stop.

"Is there something wrong? Are you in pain?"

He shook, but speech was too much effort. Summoning his remaining strength, he lifted Perori an inch or two from his chest.

"You want me to carry her?"

Palle was shocked, but the strain of this final act was too much for Easten. He sank back onto the litter, collapsing into a death-like trance from which none of Moirag's frantic ministrations could rouse him. Carefully and with an awed reverence, Palle swathed Perori in every layer of protective covering he had, and the journey continued at a cruel pace. They caught up with and passed those who had been before them when they were forced to stop and surged onwards until directly behind the scouts in the vanguard. The tang of salt air mingled with a trace of woodsmoke hinted they were close to Dubh Lyn. As they crested the next small rise, the town lay spread at their feet. A rider was despatched to alert the Council of Elders of their imminent arrival, and the urgent need of a sickbay.

CHAPTER FOURTEEN

"What do you need to treat the patient? What caused his illness?"

Moirag felt flustered, even embarrassed. The physician who addressed her was at least old enough to be her grandfather yet indicated he was prepared and willing to follow her lead in reviving Easten. He seemed to read her thoughts and smiled.

"You were with this young man when he fell ill. You observed him before the malady struck, when he was in full health, and you have at least some knowledge of what happened. Despite my years of experience I was not there, and I am not privy to the details, but they may hold the clue to his recovery!"

Grateful for the older medic's seal of approval, Moirag nodded her thanks and turned to study Easten with a touch more confidence. His outer clothing had been peeled back. He had been placed on a mattress covered with spotless white linen, raised on a table. She placed an ear on his chest, directly above the heart.

"He breathes, shallowly but without discomfort," she murmured. In truth, she could only confirm this because she could feel his chest expand and deflate. A bystander (even not touching Easten's frame) might not have noticed. "His heart beats, too, but slowly, too slowly, and his body is cool. His first and most urgent need is warmth;

blankets, and a place near a blazing hearth!"

At a discreet signal from the elder, the fire was banked up; blankets appeared, and drapes were hung around the doors and windows to block errant draughts.

"And when you have warmed him through, what then? Are there potions, herbs or other treatments you might need once he awakens?"

Moirag's head spun. There was so much to consider, and she was young. You do him no favours if you allow yourself to panic, she told herself. Calm, think! As the room warmed rapidly beads of moisture appeared on Easten's forehead. She took a clean cloth and carefully dried them. A thought struck, and she turned to the elder physician. "Forgive my impudence, Sir; I should have asked your name before I began treating the patient! But time seemed most important and…"

The mage silenced her with a gesture. "I agree with you, time is of great importance in treating this patient, and I have lived so long I can sometimes barely remember my name: no offence taken! But if you feel the urge to know, my name is Colum. Does that help with your plans to cure the patient?"

Moirag's confidence grew, though she couldn't explain why. She thought furiously for a few seconds. Slow heart, cold body… there had to be something she could do. The picture of a flower popped into her mind, and she realised this was the answer. But it was the wrong time of year. She turned again to Colum.

"Do you have in your stores the sap (or the ground, dried powder) of a plant known as the foxglove? A small, purple flower which…"

"Grows in springtime?" He nodded. "I have some small

stocks, young apothecary, but I'm unaware of any virtues of healing this plant might have! My liege lord Cormac asked me to secure a small stock for… other purposes." He didn't elaborate but allowed his glance to wander the room.

"It stimulates the heart. In a healthy heart, this can even make it race so hard, it bursts. Yet when the heart beats as slowly as Easten's, barely keeping him alive, a carefully measured small dose can restore the heart to a regular, healthy rhythm."

"And you've performed this… small miracle… just how many times?"

"This healing comes from an older, wiser source, Master; one ancient in years, compared with a brief human life. I heard it in the song of *An Trom*, the elder tree, the self-same source of much of the medicine lore I use. She whispers secrets of healing from the Earth Mother; the properties of the plants and herbs. Do you not consult her?" Moirag's brow furrowed; there was no guile or irony in her question.

Colum studied her gravely a few moments. There were clearly hidden depths in this young Healer. He nodded to an assistant and murmured a few words. "I learnt my craft from a more mortal tutor, but I am familiar with the range of remedies provided by Nature. I have also heard of other Healing practices such as you describe, but I have never met anyone who lives by them! Let us make the patient comfortable. I imagine we will have to rouse him before we can persuade him to drink the potion."

"Once I have the herbs and plants I need, I can prepare the remedy, but it will take time."

"Everything in my stockroom is at your disposal; my

assistant will help you find whatever you need."

Moirag didn't trust herself to speak, but nodded her grateful thanks to Colum and left the infirmary. A silent youth trailed in her wake, closing the door behind them.

Colum's workspace was but a few doors along the passageway from the room where Easten lay. It wasn't merely clean, but ruthlessly spartan and scrubbed; there wasn't as much as a measuring spoon or the smallest container of powdered or liquid preparation left carelessly unattended on a random surface. Everything appeared to be identified with a label (written or with pictures of the plant) and assigned a place on one of the ordered shelves and ledges running floor to ceiling around the room. The only break in the shelving was in the vicinity of the single door, and around the open-hearth fire in the long wall opposite the door. There were no windows, but Moirag felt a faint current against her cheek, and realised there must be a discreet ventilation keeping the room warm but not stuffy. There was a healthy glow to the fire and plenty of fuel, but what pleased her more was the range of pots, pans, and kettles in every size, scrupulously clean, their bright copper surfaces gleaming in ordered racks, reflecting the flames.

Moirag selected a pot she judged a suitable size, but before she could cross the room to draw water her silent assistant took it from her and went to the pump. Such menial tasks were beneath her dignity.

When he returned with the water, Moirag searched through the cornucopia of plants and herbs. She nodded her thanks, and thought she recognised a mixture of pride and pleasure in her assistant's eyes. "My thanks! What may I call you?"

The response was a gentle smile and a finger laid against his lips. Did that mean he was unable to speak, or had taken a vow of silence. She tried again. "I see you understand what I say, so I know you aren't deaf. If you have taken a vow that prevents you speaking, I will not tell anyone if you wish to break or suspend it while we work! But I will not insist on conversation if you would rather hold to your oath. Is that acceptable?"

A nod, and this time there could be no doubt about the young man's gratitude. He bowed, then busying himself with the mundane task of tending the fire, keeping the flame constant, so Moirag didn't have to soil her hands while preparing medicine.

A discreet knock on the door startled Moirag and sent her assistant scampering to answer it. There was nobody in the passageway when he opened the door, but a large wicker basket of freshly plucked foxgloves had been left, some with sap bleeding from the stems.

The fresher, the better! Moirag thought as she separated the delicate heads from their stalks. The petals would have to be stripped from the stamens later, but every part of the plant had uses—none would be wasted.

Moirag had to work carefully. A deadly poison was contained within the innocuous-looking flower, and as far as practical she avoided touching it with her hands and fingers, working with forceps, knives and other instruments. Knights and warriors had gauntlets to protect their hands and forearms, she caught herself thinking, 'tis a pity there isn't a more delicate fabric, as soft and pliant as skin. She frowned. Where had such a strange thought come from? For the moment, she must concentrate on every stage of her preparations. There was no room for error. A grain no bigger than a salt crystal might make all the difference between killer and cure… As the water in the kettle heated through, the first fumes to rise to the surface were rank and noxious; Moirag recognised them as the impurities released from the plants, a part of the distillation to be endured. She was grateful for the room's ventilation. From experience, she knew they could quickly make anyone exposed to them ill, or worse.

The powerful sickly stench dissipated, and the steam rising from the liquid remaining in the cooking vessel cleared to a healthier off-white, slightly denser than seen from a pan of pure spring water when it reaches boiling point. There was a suggestion of a scent, but this time redolent of spring flowers. Once a stream of vapour rose from the surface of the liquid in the pot Moirag reached for a hollow, V-shaped tube which it had taken minutes to locate. One end was wider than the other, and she placed this over the pot, trapping the steam.

The other end narrowed to a small hole, beneath which she placed a small glass. "Now we wait!" she murmured, and flushed as she realised she'd spoken aloud. She smiled at her silent companion and assistant. "My apologies! I often talk to myself while I work, especially if the job is difficult or delicate!"

Holding the tube at the bend, Moirag felt it heat, but not so she could no longer hold it. This was caused by the steam inside the tube, which turned back to liquid as it cooled and dripped into the glass. The liquid in the base of the glass had the faintest tinge of yellow, rather than the crystal clear of spring water. Moirag counted every drip as a blessing, keeping a tally as the volume steadily increased.

She counted seven 'hands' before the intervals between drips lengthened. One more hand (counting one finger for each drip) and she was prompted to raise the tube and peer at the remaining liquid; there was little left, and she decided that was as much as she would get from this batch.

She nodded to her helper and made a 'throw away' motion. As she lifted the glass and studied the contents, she noticed that as soon as he had emptied the remaining sludge from the base, he poured more hot water into the pot and scrubbed vigorously. She realised there was a good explanation for the pristine state of Colum's pots and pans.

She was in no doubt that what she had in her hands was certainly a potent, toxic poison. Now, with no previous experience to guide her she had to attempt a guess at how far she needed to dilute it. *This just isn't fair,* she thought, with a flutter of panic stirring in her breast. *How do I decide? If I get it wrong, I'll be responsible for my patient's death…*

She had to do something constructive. Using the smallest measure scoops she'd found, she dipped into the precious liquid and transferred it to another glass. In this, she added nine more scoops of pure water. She was fairly good with numbers and weakening it by a factor of ten was something she would remember easily.

Swirling it to mix it thoroughly, she saw that the slightly oily consistency she'd noticed in the undiluted fluid had disappeared. The yellowy colour, however, was unchanged.

She took a metal spoon and dipped it into the diluted mix for seconds, then withdrew and studied it closely, first with her eyes, then holding it under her nose. Finally, she held it close to her ear, listening for any indication of 'fizz' or chemical reaction. Nothing.

She repeated the process with a glass rod, then a wooden peg. The peg remained damp: it wasn't waxed or lacquered, so some liquid was bound to seep into the grain. Other than that, the results appeared identical; no reactions.

The next step was potentially the most dangerous: using it on a living subject. There was only one option: she had to test it on herself.

The wooden peg still had residual dampness. Holding her breath in terror (and anticipation of pain) she laid it gently on the tender, sensitive skin of her wrist.

Was that a faint tingle, or nothing more than the dampness expected from the experiment? She lifted the peg and concentrated on her wrist, ready to plunge her arm into a pail of fresh water at a suspicion of a blister or other deformity.

It was a welcome anticlimax, she realised that this 'nothing' was the most encouraging result she could hope for.

"Courage! You are brave to test the potion thus. But the taste will be bitter: you must needs disguise it!"

Moirag caught her breath. The voice was clear in her head, but unfamiliar. Her assistant showed no reaction, and it wasn't a young man's voice. She stared at him but knew he hadn't spoken. Slowly she raised the wooden peg once more and touched it gingerly to the tip of her tongue. Yes, there was an immediate bitterness, and the most sensitive cells in her body were deadened, but she sensed no danger.

Fruit juices or wine; a sweet wine, she decided. Surely that was the easiest way to hide the bitterness. And a suitable drinking vessel; not a glass, too easy to drop and smash, ruining all her hard work. A cup, perhaps, or a goblet since she'd decided to use wine to camouflage the taste…

"Can you find me wine? I need to sweeten the potion, to help my patient swallow the draught."

The acolyte nodded and led her to a corner of the room, where a dozen or more bottles lay flat on a rack, some covered in a thin layer of dust. Moirag assumed these were of an earlier vintage, probably sweeter than the others. She plucked one at random and wiped the dust from the surface, revealing a label with numbers: she didn't recognise numbers with more than two digits, and had to assume it was a date.

Close to the left of the wine rack was a small cabinet. The door was slightly ajar, and Moirag glimpsed what she hoped for. A drinking vessel, pewter or silver, covered with engravings. She knew her letters, but much of the design seemed to consist of symbols she didn't recognise. It was reasonably clean, which was her main concern, and comfortably big enough to hold the potion.

Carefully, she decanted the diluted medicine into the… cup? Chalice seemed a more appropriate term. She added half the bottle of wine: almost as an afterthought, she decided to take the remainder of the bottle with her.

"Take me back to Colum; we must persuade the patient to drink this while fresh."

Covering the goblet with a cloth, Moirag turned and headed for the door. Her assistant had anticipated her request and led her swiftly along the corridor.

"You work swiftly, Healer!" Colum greeted. Moirag was startled. She'd been concentrating so hard on her appointed task she had no idea how much (or little) time had passed.

"The medicine is fresh, and sweetened with this wine: I found it by chance. I really should have asked your leave to use it, but…"

"When I said you could use anything to hand, little one, I meant it sincerely. If you have managed to concoct an elixir that revives our honoured guest, the loss of a single bottle (even of the finest vintage) is a small price!"

Easten was still deathly cold to the touch. Moirag was concerned and called for more blankets. She chafed his hands, massaging them to stimulate his blood flow. Some of the blue tinge disappeared from his fingertips, but not swiftly enough to satisfy her.

"There is one more thing we can attempt," she murmured.

"So tell us, Healer; anything that may help, and anything we can do to assist you, you have but to name it!"

"Remove his outer clothing, move the bed closer to the hearth fire."

"Remove his outer clothing? Won't that cause him to freeze even more?"

"No, my Lord. Not if I follow suit and lay next to him in the bed. If another is prepared to do the same, and lie behind him at the same time, we can transfer our body warmth to Easten twice as fast. This is something I learned from our village huntsman, who discovered the trick on a midwinter hunt."

Palle had needed no second bidding. He was already stripped to his undergarments. "What are we waiting for?"

Moirag removed her outer cloak slowly, hoping she wasn't offending anyone by displaying more of her svelte figure and flawless skin than was custom. She didn't spot a lustful or lascivious gleam in any eye, nor hear any intake of breath or lewd comments, but she was past caring what others think. Her sole concern was for the recovery of 'her' patient, and for the moment this seemed the best way forward. She folded her dress to use as an improvised pillow, and silently indicated Palle do the same. As soon as the bed had been moved close to the hearth, yet a safe distance from falling embers, further blankets were brought and piled over and round the warming huddle of three.

Two attendants stood fire watch. A priest knelt in the privacy of the far corner and reached for his Missal; the remainder of the court followed Cormac out of the room. Moirag laid her cheek against Easten's. It was still deathly cold, but her ears told her he was breathing. All she could see of Palle was a tangle of curls, but this was enough to confirm he had spooned his chest against Easten's back, facing her. Nothing more could be done but wait—or join Fr. Tomàs in prayer, if one's beliefs favoured the new religion. A further layer of blankets arrived, and Moirag signalled someone to dry the perspiration forming on her brow, and presumably on Palle's. For the moment, Easten's body remained obstinately cold, with no sign of sweats on his face.

The fire was stoked as needed, but all other sound and movement in the room ceased. If Fr. Tomàs was praying or reading Scripture, he was doing so silently. Perhaps half an hour passed of near-total silence. Moirag felt calmer: this peaceful interlude was what she needed after her physical and mental exertions preparing the untested draught.

It was so tempting to drift, let her body relax into the natural sleep it demanded, build a fresh reserve of energy. Later, she told herself, firmly. Rest is a luxury you cannot allow yourself yet: look, listen, feel, observe. You have much still to learn of the art of healing.

This mild, not-quite-admonishment rang in her ears, and once again it seemed she was listening to well-meant advice from an older, wiser mentor. The voice in her ears was not hers. Without doubt it seemed that of an older man.

And there was a change in Easten, but not in the extreme ends of his fingertips, which she had thought the logical place to check for returning warmth and vitality, nor in the cheek still in direct contact with hers. She was aware of a stronger, more rapid flow of blood pulsating from Easten's chest, strong enough for her to feel it throb against her breast as they lay, entwined as lovers in a marriage bed. Warmth percolated, slowly, but definitively, outward from the central point occupied by his heart. It took a minute or two before her cheek confirmed the prayed-for, much-needed return of warm, life-giving blood to Easten's upper body. Palle had also sensed a change in the comatose victim, who showed signs of fighting his way out of the shadows, towards consciousness. He slid from under the mountain of blankets, and without pausing to dress himself snatched a cloth from the nearest bench to wipe the beads of perspiration at long last appearing on Easten's brow.

Soon it was possible for two strong warriors to support Easten in a semi-upright position. His eyes were clear, his skin taking a more natural hue.

"You must try to swallow this draught, and trust in *An Trom*! She it was who told me to prepare this for you, and she has saved you once today already."

Easten nodded and took his medicine without protest. The taste was not unpleasant; Moirag had used sufficient sweeteners. "He is still weak, we must be patient, and allow him rest…"

The words seemed to be coming from a vast distance. Easten couldn't even identify the speaker's voice as male or female. As soon as the potion had passed his lips he felt a glow of health spread through his body, warming his chest even before it reached his stomach. He sagged against the arms of his supporters, and felt a cool cloth pressed to his forehead but was unaware of the extra blanket draped across him a few seconds later, as oblivion closed around him and allowed his defences to begin the painstaking process of repairing his body.

Moirag tucked the uppermost blanket over Easten's shoulder, noting with satisfaction his breathing was easier, more natural. She felt a twinge in her back, reminding her of the time she had spent bent almost double over her patient. She stretched to encourage her muscles into their accustomed position and noticed Cormac and Fr. Tomàs were studying the cup she'd used to administer the medicine. They had their heads close and seemed deep in private conversation. She hesitated, but Cormac glanced in her direction and beckoned her with an encouraging smile.

"I was careful with the cup, Sire!" she blurted as she approached. "I could see it was old, and decorated with precious gems… "

"And you handled it carefully, as befits any ancient object! It is undamaged, as you can see, you did no wrong. When I said you could use anything you found in my rooms, I meant it! Yet it is interesting you chose this chalice to administer the healing draught you concocted, which seems to be working as we speak!"

He gestured to Easten. Even at a distance, the improvement was visible.

Fr. Tomàs lifted the chalice with an unmistakeable reverence usually associated with a sacred vessel or a saint's relics. A frisson of panic caused Moirag's heart to skip a beat. Had she ventured onto unsafe ground, transgressed some ancient and inviolable religious convention?

The priest looked away from the chalice and gazed deep into her eyes. "Fear not, child. You have done no wrong, committed no sin. How could healing another ever be considered a wrongful deed?"

He had clearly sensed the root of Moirag's unease. He smiled at her again and lifted the chalice almost as if he had decided to use it for a blessing or absolution. Cormac stirred and extended his hand. Fr. Tomàs paused, then responded to the tacit request by offering it to the king for closer inspection.

As Cormac's fingers touched the chalice every detail of the etchings covering it blazed into life, a tracery network of molten silver veins that coursed the outer surface, swirling and dancing the rim to the broad, wide base, transforming it in an instant from an inanimate, functional drinking vessel to an exceptionally beautiful and unique object, filled with the promise of health and vitality. The microscopic threads of the etchings pulsed, bringing the chalice to life.

Moirag's Healer instincts were never far from her conscious thoughts. Her reaction was to note that Cormac's rough, calloused hands and the ancient parchment-thin skin of Fr. Tomàs' fingers was without question smoother, more even, resembling a far younger man's, in the prime of youth.

The etchings on the chalice continued to pulse and flux. A question formed in a dark corner of Moirag's mind: she heard her own voice asking, but it sounded faint, as if coming from an unimaginably great distance, yet every word, every syllable was clear and distinct. "What do these symbols mean? I know my letters, but there are many signs I have never seen…"

"I can tell you little of that," Cormac admitted. "As Clan Chief I am first and foremost a warrior, and never had cause to learn my letters! Perhaps our Priest can unfold this mystery. All I can offer is that when my grandsire entrusted the cup to me, he said it was already ancient when he in turn received it from his grandsire. How it came to be a family heirloom is lost in the mists of time."

Fr. Tomàs studied the silver fire flowing across the goblet's smooth surface. "The engravings are for the most part lettering," he said, "but the words they form are in a mixture of languages. I recognise Latin and Greek, but there are other letters—signs, perhaps?—I do not recognise…"

He traced his forefinger along a thread that ended at the base of a slight but distinctive lip on the vessel's rim. Directly across it was a bulb just beneath the rim, suggesting a handle to make pouring easier. He froze, his finger glued to the surface. Moirag peered closely, her heart hammering wildly with anticipation. The symbol was etched below the pouring lip on the rim.

"This symbol is from a language older than Latin, but dates from when the Romans persecuted the early Church. It is formed of two Greek letters, chi and rho, used as a sign of identity among early believers, as they are the first letters of The Lord's name, Kristus."

"And although I know my letters—possibly better than most!—there are symbols I have never come across. They may be older than Greek, they may not be letters but signs, pictures, who can tell?"

"How can this chalice be as old as you suggest?" Moirag wanted to know.

"See! It is unblemished, unmarked, as if fresh from a smithy's workbench! The jewels, too: when they catch the light they sparkle, as if freshly quarried!"

"Cormac has told us what he knows of the chalice's history, before it came to him: and if you had known of its likely origin and history, my Lord, you might have thought hard about allowing your physician to mix potions in it! It's clear that, despite its fresh, newly forged appearance this vessel is old: very old."

"Moirag, we both saw what happened when the chalice was placed into the king's hands…"

"Yes, Father, the letters… "

"Indeed! That was when we first saw the letters, which must have been there all the time, awaiting some power to make them visible. I believe it is no coincidence you chose this drinking vessel. And indeed, if I am right, no other cup in the history of the world could be more fitting for healing someone."

Fr. Tomàs knelt before Cormac, hands clasped in prayer. "Sire, with all my heart I believe this is a precious and powerful object, lost for countless years. The etchings and arcane symbols in several ancient languages, and the healing processes we have witnessed suggest this chalice could be the cup known as the Holy Grail."

CHAPTER FIFTEEN

Cormac accepted the offer of accommodation for himself and a handful of senior officers but refused a general invitation to the remainder of the party.

"'Twould be a discourtesy to expect the hospitality of the town to be extended to two hundred extra mouths," he insisted, " and we cannot yet be certain how many days we may be here before continuing our journey."

He issued instructions for the party to set up camp outside the fortified barrow protecting the delightfully disorganised streets and alleys that ran with no attempt at order throughout Dubh Lyn. As the last light faded, dozens of small cooking fires blossomed as evening meals were prepared from the field rations each man carried.

Palle had no specific role. With Easten unconscious (and well attended by three physicians and their acolytes) he was ignored and frustrated. Part of him wanted to strip back Perori's outer cladding, using the music to get through to the unconscious bard. To occupy his mind he strolled the courtyard that fronted the main entrance. It was a respectable size, as many as seven hundred warriors bristling with every personal weapon imaginable had assembled there, but Palle felt constricted. At the main gate he paused and looked across the wooden bridge, which could be swiftly raised on chains, creating an impassable moated channel serviced by the river running south of the township, supplying residents with clean, refreshing drinking water as well as a natural defence.

Silent and unmoving on the far bank was a group of figures curiously difficult to define. Four were in a perfect square around a central fifth. They seemed to hover inches above the grass and made no attempt to cross the bridge.

Sí, and the band of Fae! How could he have forgotten to provide for their otherworldly companions? They had not been invited along with Cormac and his officers; they had never been considered part of the 'fighting force', and equally didn't belong to the 'other ranks' billeted on the eaves of the nearby woods. In his arms, Perori sighed a lugubrious tone, though Palle was certain he hadn't jostled or disturbed her.

"Easy, friend: we are not offended! You have had much to think about, many tasks to perform since arriving here on the easternmost shores of the realm!"

Palle had to assume the comment he 'heard' in his inner ear were from Sí, the only one of the Fae who had communicated directly with any of the party. The words came quietly, a private message murmured for him alone, not as if they had been called from the distance of at least two hundred yards on the opposite side of the protective moat. It might have been his imagination, but it seemed to Palle there was a barely suppressed dry humour bubbling just beyond Sí's greeting. Stories about the Sídhe having an almost childlike humour were not, without basis. He tried to gather his wits, wondering with one corner of his mind if he needed to reply or simply marshal his thoughts and 'send' them.

Before he could decide, Sí's voice sounded again. "You're a quick pupil, apprentice Bard! There's no need to fill your lungs or inform the rest of the world—especially when you carry the lute. I sense your given name is Palle, and the lute's present player has named her Perori. These labels suffice."

Sí nodded, to indicate Palle reply. His instinct was to make amends for the failure to include the Sídhe in the hospitality arrangements. "How can I… we?"

"Provide sustenance, or lodging? That will not be necessary, and even if it were, I sense it would not be possible. We are not comfortable in stiff, solid, hand-built halls and houses. Bothy or barony, cottage, or castle, makes us ill at ease. There is a 'wrongness' in the carved and worked wood used to construct the bridge separating us that would cause us discomfort to tread upon! And we take all the nourishment we need from the bounty of Mother Earth; sustenance from the soil, water from her rivers, air which flows freely all around."

"So there is nothing we can offer you for comfort?"

"Laughter, and song! Rest easy, Bard apprentice! Our needs are few, and beyond your abilities to provide! We will also watch through the night, so all concerned may rest. This message you may carry to he who leads the township, and to his guest, King Cormac. Sleep well, there is much still to be accomplished before you take to the ships to complete your journey."

The five figures swayed, brightening perceptibly as if drawing the last rays of the dying sun into their semi-solid forms. Away from the town's walls they drifted and fanned into a neat arc halfway between the moat and the encampment of Cormac's band, nestled against the forest flanks. Silence settled over the town and fields, soothing even the least experienced young warrior (of which there were quite a few being 'blooded'), allowing everyone to take advantage of the chance to sleep the night untroubled by fears of an attack.

CHAPTER SIXTEEN

Easten drifted as the effects of the medicine spread. Murmurs of conversation blurred into an indistinct rumble of vague, soothing sounds. A delicious glow of warmth coursed his veins, and he could hear his heart beating more rapidly, stronger, eager to carry blood enriched with the healing draught to every part of his body. He made no attempt to stir—he didn't think movement would be possible. He was no longer conscious of physical contact with his bed, or the room's temperature. His body was numb, but his mind fully conscious. For some reason, this did not disquiet him; he sensed that to be effective, the medication administered demanded a quiescent, unresisting body.

A figure swam slowly almost into focus. The form blurred, but the crown of russet mane suggested Moirag stood over him and extended the fingers of a hand.

"Sleep now."

He couldn't feel the contact she made with the normally sensitive skin of his eyelids, but when a pattern of loops and sworls in a rainbow of colours danced, he realised she had closed his eyes for him. Until that moment, he'd been unaware of the paralysis (temporary, he hoped) brought about by the powerful drug he'd swallowed. He didn't even have the self-control to perform such a simple operation without Moirag's intervention.

"Rest, Master Colum; 'tis only fair I should take first watch over our patient."

The words floated slowly through Easten's consciousness, but he was unable to decide if they had been spoken aloud. He could only be certain they were spoken in Moirag's distinctive, slightly husky contralto.

He sensed rather than 'heard' Colum's grunt of acceptance, and after seconds knew somehow he was alone in the room with the young Healer responsible for saving his life. One sense unaffected by the paralysing medicine was his hearing. This was enhanced. He was acutely aware of every rustle of clothing as Moirag moved, each crackle and hiss from the turf burning in the hearth; even his own slow, steady breathing was as loud as a fierce autumn gale.

His active mind made his inability to communicate with the person who had saved his life doubly frustrating. He felt a slow rage coagulate deep inside his head, which was good: he might be unable to move, but he could still feel emotion! The rage in his breast grew, a warm glow, loosening stiff, frozen muscles as his heart pumped more strongly. His hypersensitive inner ear confirmed the steadily increasing tempo as the blood coursing his veins brought his body to life. He concentrated desperately to force any bodily function to respond, so Moirag might see. Eyelids, fingertips, toes, nostrils, anything…

A cool (hand? cloth?) on his fevered brow! Success!

"Easten? Can you hear me?"

A reaction! He couldn't tell which of his efforts had succeeded attracting his saviour's attention, but his relief was overwhelming. He redoubled his efforts, concentrating on one task. He channelled his energy into one grand gesture, and consciously willed his eyelids to flutter. They felt as heavy as lead; solid, unmoving slabs of granite.

"Are you awake? Are you trying to reach out to me?"

Fighting with every ounce of strength, he concentrated once more on forcing his eyelids to react. The tiniest flash of... something, other than total darkness? ...was he mistaken? The sensation of a cooling cloth or hand once more, this time against his eyelids. Slight pressure applied, then removed...

A supreme effort, and this time his eyelids cracked apart. He couldn't control the tiny muscles needed to focus, identify the details of his surroundings, but he could identify the shifting shadows and flickerings from the hearth.

"Easten, *ma cushla*, can you hear me? You mustn't fight the power of the medicine! But if you decide to fight me, with the healing, that can only be good!"

Slowly he forced his eyelids closed, then open once more. They felt like dry, gritty cloths trampled on a dusty floor, grating on the surface of his eyeballs. Blurred motion close to his head: yet he was unable to focus his vision. Seconds later Moirag was in close attendance once more, whispering encouragement and endearments in his ear as she bathed his eyes with warm, rose-tinted water. He identified the flower's familiar perfume; another sense awakening. He tested this by consciously making his nostrils flare and twitch.

A second small miracle! Deliberately, he pulled as hard as he could to fill his lungs as far as possible through his nose. When he could take no more on board, he deliberately held the air in his lungs as long as he could before releasing it through his mouth and lips.

"Don't work too hard: the medicine needs time to have its full effect!" Moirag cautioned. "Let us play a game, one I do not believe will tire you! All you must do is twitch your nose. Once for "Yes", twice for "No". Can you manage that?"

Twitch.

"Good! I'll ask you questions, and you can answer Yes or No… Let me see, where to start …? Do you feel pain?"

Twitch, twitch.

"Good—at least, I think so! Do you feel anything?"

Twitch, twitch.

"Not even this damp cloth, on your face?"

A slight pause: then once again a negative response.

"My hand on your arm?" She let him see she was pinching his forearm: quite hard, leaving a small bruise when she released. A longer pause. Easten seemed to be considering the options before he replied with a double twitch. This time he seemed to want to take the initiative and forced himself to blink his eyes. Moirag paused in her one-sided questioning, unsure what Easten expected.

He was gradually becoming aware of a certain sensation restoring itself in his face, spreading from his eyes and nostrils, unfreezing the tiny muscles around his lips, chin, cheeks and forehead, unwaxing his stiff features that had reduced him to a helpless caricature, a corpselike statue held in stasis by the power of the drugs he'd ingested. He suspected the "kill or cure" medicine Moirag had brewed for his treatment had come close to ending his life before its benefits had resulted in the desired effect.

Easten, however, was too impatient to wait for his body to thaw out. The thud and pulse of blood flowing more strongly past his eardrums told him the healing process had begun, but the rejuvenation was happening far too slowly.

He forced himself to take as deep a breath as his still-frozen chest muscles would permit. Deliberately, he formed a ball of rage deep in his consciousness, spreading to all points of an imaginary compass placed in the region of his heart. He willed the heat of the savage emotion to act on every muscle, cartilage, flesh and bone as it circulated in his veins, arteries, and down to the most delicate network of blood capillaries pumping life blood back to every part of his body.

It took a superhuman effort, but he commanded the muscles of his neck to contort sufficiently for him to turn his head a few significant degrees to the left. Moirag's head and shoulders swam into view, but he still had no control over the fine adjustment muscles controlling the focus of his vision. He was certain she had one hand on either his wrist or chest, checking his vital signs, but as yet he couldn't feel anything below his throat.

Easten's strenuous, determined efforts could only produce a minimal reaction, but it was enough to catch Moirag's attention.

"Are you in pain?"

Her voice was full of concern. Easten tried to force a sound, even a grunt through his throat but it was still too constricted: he had to fall back on the agreed silent signal.

Twitch, twitch.

Not strictly true: feeling was returning in various parts of his body. Pins and needles stabbed mercilessly, as if a million soldier ants had descended on his defenceless form, voraciously feeding, stripping flesh clean from bones.

Moirag's face swam in and out of focus as Easten strove to regain a degree of independence in the muscles of his fingers and toes. He told himself, if he could only feel something in his extremities, he could expect sensation and control to return to other parts of his body. She leaned over his once more, and he felt the coolness of the damp cloth she laid across his brow.

"You burn, still!" she whispered. "What can I do to help?"

She broke off, whirling on the balls of her feet as the door burst open behind her. Palle entered, cradling Perori. "Your pardon, milady! The cry was urgent, and Perori..." he hesitated, holding the lute before him on his open palms. His fingers weren't even close to touching the strings but nervous, plangent discords hummed and clashed in the confines of the room, desperately seeking a harmonious resolution.

Drawing on every reserve of willpower, Easten concentrated his efforts into forcing a reaction into his fingertips. He felt—or thought he felt—the tiniest movement, but couldn't be certain...

Both Palle and Moirag studied the patient closely.

Palle was first to react. "I believe he's asking me..."

He moved to the bedside and laid the precious instrument on Easten's breast, curling the still-frozen fingers of his left hand around the fingerboard, then placing the bard's right hand across Perori's belly.

The harsh, unmusical, jagged clashes resolved into a shimmering, triumphal major chord. A heartbeat later

Easten's fingers lost their waxy stiffness and pallor, softening as blood was pumped through his body and his skin took on a more natural hue. His eyelids fluttered and his chest rose as he took a long, slow breath, filling his air-starved lungs. The blood vessels in his neck stood out, a deep purple against the still-pale skin of his throat as they worked overtime to force oxygen-rich blood through his brain and other vital organs.

Easten flexed his fingers: his left hand reconfigured to stop the strings, and his right hand brushed the soundbox, scattering a sweet arpeggio of notes across the room, almost visible. His eyes remained closed as his fingers moved to a different chord, then another before segueing into a satisfying final cadence, hanging in the air for seconds before winking out of existence. His eyes snapped open: clear, sparkling with renewed health and energy. He smiled, but made no attempt to rise from the table unaided. His breathing had become free and easy, and his skin tone was now a healthy shade of summer tanned healthy pink.

"A hot drink—or, better, broth!" Moirag took charge and nobody thought to query the Healer's right to issue orders.

"He needs something to help him regain strength and to be moved so he can sit up and swallow…"

*

Easten was carefully transferred from his supine table position to a couch that allowed him to recline in a near-upright position close to the fire. Moirag fussed until satisfied he was covered with a sufficiency of wraps, shawls and blankets.

"You'll have to place Perori on one side while you sup the broth!" she said, with a mock scold.

Easten glared at her and seemed on the point of arguing the point.

"You don't want to risk staining her with an accidental spill, do you?"

"Then find furniture that can be padded with this overload of blankets and place her within my reach!"

Moirag nodded and stooped to spoonfeed Easten the broth. His left hand caressed Perori's fretboard as he ate, feeling the broth's warmth restore him.

"Your recovery was so rapid, it seemed miraculous," said Fr. Tomàs. "I choose the word carefully! For in this instance, I mean it sincerely.

"When you were first brought here, your life signs were so weak, I thought I might be called on to administer the Last Rites! It seems my vigil of prayer was not totally in vain, but I am in no doubt your wondrous instrument…"

"Your pardon, Father: I have come to think of Perori as my Companion. As far as I'm concerned, she has a life of her own; I am privileged to share each day I spend with her."

"We all saw—and heard!—something special here tonight," Palle offered. "It began while you were still as cold as death. As soon as I laid Perori on your breast she breathed a musical phrase, though no hand touched her strings. I could swear the notes that danced around the room were so full of life, I could almost see them!" He looked from the priest to the Healer, begging for confirmation. Both nodded.

"There's no doubt in my mind, young man: your

recovery began the moment your instr… pardon! your 'companion' was laid across your body." Father Tomàs affirmed. "Your colour, your breathing, all signs that you could still be counted among the living. Everything began that moment, and Palle is right: the music was so vibrant, I could almost taste it, smell it!"

Easten signalled to Moirag that he could eat no more and reached for his beloved companion. He froze at the priest's words, holding Perori mid-air. He had a puzzled frown."Doesn't everyone? Music must be more than a mere jumble of notes. Surely you must feel it, the life it brings, the laughter, the peace?"

The unquestioning, almost childlike sincerity in his voice and his puzzled look might have caused an amused or facetious comment, but it was clear Easten was speaking from the heart and meant each word. Palle was the first to react; as a musician, he had some understanding of what Easten was trying to say.

"My musical skills are modest compared to yours, my friend, but I have felt the same way, from time to time. Music has indeed a magical quality!"

"And none of us could be in any doubt as to how quickly you recovered, once Perori was laid on your chest," Fr. Tomàs added. "But perhaps we should simply be grateful for this minor miracle and discuss our next move. We were pursued on the final stage of our trek from Moylurg. We cannot remain here long! Even if we escape unchallenged, whoever hunts us may vent their wrath on Dubh Lyn!"

"And they will discover that it is no easy mark: for you will be under our protection!" Sí drifted from the shadows in one corner of the room, catching them all by surprise.

Even Easten hadn't been aware of her nebulous presence. A stirring in the air behind her suggested the presence of her brothers.

Palle took a step backwards, and Fr. Tomàs crossed himself.

"Peace, friends! Sí and her brothers are the only reason we made it to Dubh Lyn unscathed! The Fianna are as real as we, not mere legends for children! If she says they will remain and offer protection, be certain they will not fail you—though I confess, I had not expected you to offer yourselves as a fighting force!" Easten concluded, with a respectful nod towards the Færy spokesperson.

Sí smiled. "In that, you are right! We do not 'fight' in the sense you understand. All forms of violence are alien to our way of life. But we can throw your opponents into confusion, lead them a merry dance, trick them until they know not which way to turn! That will give you the breathing space to assemble your troops and get them safely aboard the ships waiting for you!"

"Then we should make our move swiftly, during what remains of the night!" Easten affirmed, rising to his feet. He layered Perori's protective valise and skins around the precious instrument. Without waiting for a command, Palle slipped out of the room to inform the officers in charge of the troops, and make sure the crews of the longships were ready to receive them.

*

Cormac's troops were assembled by murmured word and silent signal. Easten led the way to the harbour, where Erik awaited.

"Two hundred warriors? Impressive, friend Easten! They move on cat paws. I've known raiding parties of a dozen seasoned Vikings make more noise! Do you bring me a fighting force of ghosts?"

Easten, for all his lack of military experience, had been conscious of how swiftly and silently the loaned forces had mustered.

"I believe that may be in some part due to the influence of our most recent allies, several of the Fianna: a folk who describe themselves as 'in this world, but not of it'. More detailed explanations must wait until we are safely away, but I can tell you this much, they are not bound by the same strict rules of Time as we mortals. That much they have demonstrated in the few days since we met them. Now it seems they are also able to conceal and cloak both sound and movement. The star map in the heavens has stood still since… I know not how long, but it hasn't changed as far as I can tell since before we passed the word to leave the tents standing as if occupied and assemble at the quayside."

"This is something else which sounds almost like sorcery."

Easten shook his head. "The Fianna are a pure folk. Mischievous perhaps, at times, as a child might be, but never malicious or evil! Their spokesperson—the only one who has 'spoken' to me, if that's the right word!—has stated that they do not fight, it is not in their nature to harm another, whatever the circumstance! Their ploy is to delay, trick, mislead and confuse, creating chaos and mayhem without inflicting injury. They will seek to prevent those who have pursued us from pressing closer until it is too late, and they will also ensure you are not attacked when they discover that we are gone!"

"We have indeed heard of these secretive Otherworld beings from time to time," Erik admitted, "but I had never thought to encounter them! Yet you tell me they have helped you, and I sense you speak truly!

"He glanced up to read the stars in the cloudless sky.

"I had noticed the slow changes in the movement of the stars. I wondered if some devilry might be afoot, as I need them to navigate my ship! If, as you say, these Færy beings can ignore the normal passing of Time, that's enough explanation for me—if I can rely on the stars to seek passage eastwards, and the rising of the sun in her accustomed place when the new day dawns! By then, we will be safe from pursuit. Welcome aboard, Master Musician; I believe you're about to become one of the last to embark!"

Easten looked around and realised that somehow the whole of the fighting force had filed past in silence while they had talked. One practical thought occurred; he turned, and was about to ask where the Harbourmaster might be when Simon stepped forwards, as if in response to Easten calling his name.

"Cormac may send a party to ride these horses back to Moylurg, but if you have need of them to defend yourselves in the coming days I'm sure he'll not take it amiss…"

Simon nodded.

"I had decided to send a swift message with a rider once we are sure the danger is past, but Cormac Rú's generosity will be acknowledged and returned with thanks! Now, Master Lutenist, 'tis time for you and your wondrous companion to depart!"

"Fare well, my friend: and God speed you back to Cymru and the beleaguered Lord Caradoc! May his brother's men strike hard for the honour and pride of Erin!"

Erik welcomed Easten aboard and slid the gangplank aside as unseen hands released the last mooring line and the longship eased from the quay to join the other vessel, already unfurling its sails in open water. A faint pallor on the horizon suggested where the sun would soon reappear, an approximate easterly bearing they would follow. The layers of soft cloth and protective wraps Easten had lovingly secured around Perori were enough to ensure few heard the majestic sequence of chords she sounded without assistance from her bearer, but Easten could feel the vibrations throughout his body, beginning from his sensitive fingertips, progressing to the deepest roots of his hair, causing a tingle on the soles of his feet.

The exertions of the past days caught up with Easten. He was physically drained. He had succeeded in carrying out the task given by his liege lord, and allowed himself to think he had done this more quickly and efficiently than he had any right to hope. Could he now deliver the troops Caradoc needed, before it was too late? Time alone would tell.

www.ingramcontent.com/pod-product-compliance
Ingram Content Group UK Ltd.
Pitfield, Milton Keynes, MK11 3LW, UK
UKHW041806090226
467841UK00002B/50